——— BREAKAWAY

BREAKAWAY

Kimberley Griffiths Little

AVON BOOKS NEW YORK

This is a work of fiction. Names, characters, places
and incidents either are the product of the author's
imagination or are used fictitiously. Any resemblance
to actual events, locales, organizations, or persons,
living or dead, is entirely coincidental and beyond
the intent of either the author or the publisher.

AVON BOOKS
A division of
The Hearst Corporation
1350 Avenue of the Americas
New York, New York 10019

Copyright © 1997 by Kimberley Griffiths Little
Interior design by Kellan Peck
Visit our website at http://AvonBooks.com
ISBN: 0-380-97488-6

Library of Congress Cataloging in Publication Data:

Little, Kimberley Griffiths.
    Breakaway / Kimberley Griffiths Little.
        p. cm
Summary: Sixth-grader Luke, who never got a chance to know his father, is convinced that he can follow in his footsteps as a great soccer player, but he finds
that success takes more than good genes.
[1. Soccer—Fiction. 2. Fathers and sons—Fiction.] I. Tttle.
PZ7.L72256Br 1997   96-41690
[Fic]—dc20   CIP

First Avon Books Printing: August 1997

Printed in the U.S.A.

FIRST EDITION

RRD   10 9 8 7 6 5 4 3 2 1

To my husband, Rusty,
for his unfailing love and encouragement,
and to my three sons,
Aaron, Jared, and Adam

May all your dreams become realities . . .

ONE

Luke Espinosa gripped the chain-link fence with both hands. His sweaty shirt stuck to the middle of his back. His legs trembled from running down the ditch banks trying to get to the fields on time. But he was too late for the kickoff. Luke shook the fence, making it rattle. He was *always* late.

By the time he got to the village soccer field, he was usually panting like Mr. Perea's hound dog who often followed him after school.

A wet nose nuzzled his hand, and Luke smiled when he saw the dog standing patiently at his feet, tail wagging. He rubbed Rex's floppy ears. "At least I don't drool like you."

Old Rex plopped on the grass, ribs heaving.

"Worn out, boy?" Luke asked. "You're too old to be following me. You know I never get to play. But someday, Rex. I don't know how, but someday I'm going to play soccer better than the whole Falcon team put together."

His grip on the fence tightened as he studied the players. Coach Pickerell divided up the Fighting Falcons into two groups, five on each side, to have a practice scrimmage. Paul Pickerell headed up one group and Tomás Abeyta the other. Paul was captain of the Fighting Falcons this year. His sandy hair glistened in the bright sun. Luke noticed the boy's leg muscles flex under his shin guards. Paul's thin face looked hungry when it came to soccer.

Coach Pickerell talked to the boys as he lined them up, putting a big hand on their shoulders. Luke was dying to know what the man was saying to them. How would it be to have your own father coach? Everybody in the city league knew the Fighting Falcons were the best team and Coach Pickerell the best coach. Paul had to be the luckiest boy in the sixth grade.

Luke scratched his damp, itchy shoulders. When he was younger he used to dream about his father a lot, even though he couldn't remember him. Some days he'd come home from school and pretend his father would be sitting there, the newspaper in one hand and the TV remote in the other. But it was just a dream.

Across the field he spotted Mr. Sanchez, the school principal, leaning against the fence. The principal was the community coordinator for the soccer teams and often watched the practices and games.

Luke craned his neck as Tomás Abeyta retrieved the ball with his toe and dribbled down the sidelines. Luke could never decide which player he'd rather be most like—Paul or Tomás. Paul had more showy, fancy moves, but Tomás never missed a play. Tomás's long, straight black hair flapped in the wind as he ran. Right on his tail, Paul caught up, but Tomás gave the red-

and-white ball a sharp kick to the right, aiming it to his forward players.

Luke sucked in his breath as Paul circled to intercept. The captain's toe caught the leather ball and halted it on the grass. He turned, and with one swift blow Paul returned the ball down the field back to his own scrimmage team.

Running down the sidelines, Coach Pickerell shouted directions.

A forward on Tomás's team chest-trapped the ball and broke from the running pack, racing full speed toward the goal.

"Breakaway," Luke whispered enviously as the player ran freely, kicking the ball forward with every stride. The next instant he groaned as the boy stumbled, grabbing at the ball with his toe while trying to maintain his balance.

Paul's team quickly caught up and the ball was lost in a scuffle of legs and feet as each team tried to recover its advantage.

Coach Pickerell blew sharply on his whistle.

Luke rested his forehead against the chain-link fence. Just watching the moves made his legs tighten, his heart race. He could imagine the hard leather ball against his toe, feel the kicks, the pass, and then the long drive down the line.

The whistle spurted again and the boys clustered around Coach Pickerell.

The ball lay on the grass. It took every ounce of Luke's willpower to keep from running out on the field. He wanted to dribble the ball and drive it right between the daydreaming goalie's legs. He imagined the net stretching and bouncing as it received the force of the ball and the winning point.

But he stayed behind the backstop fence, feeling alone and invisible.

It was worse now that Anthony had moved. They used to come to the soccer fields together to watch the teams practice. Even though Anthony played basketball on the city teams in the winter, he usually was able to come with Luke to watch the soccer. They'd lay on the lawn and chew grass and analyze the players.

Last September, Anthony's dad suddenly took a transfer with the Rainbow Bread company and moved to Los Angeles. Luke was still trying to get over the shock. Without Anthony, it seemed as if every other boy his age played soccer. Everybody except Luke. And now he didn't even have anybody to talk to.

Old Rex had become his best friend since Anthony left. Sometimes it was as if the old hound knew how Luke was feeling and didn't want him to be alone.

Luke glanced down and saw Rex's big brown eyes watching him. Then the dog slurped the back of his hand and Luke shook his head, sighing. This dog could melt your heart.

Coach Pickerell clapped his hands, and the Fighting Falcons scattered out on the field again.

Luke reached down and pulled a sticky blade of grass out of a clump growing at the base of the fence. He stuck it in his dry mouth, worked the tangy green grass for a minute, then spit it onto the dirt.

He watched two more plays, then stuck his hands

on his hips. It was time to go home. Time to fix dinner. Time to check on Mr. Perea.

Luke gave the sagging chain-link fence a farewell shove. Rex rose slowly to his feet like an old man. The dog followed Luke as he walked the rear perimeter of the field, back to the ditch road, passing a group of girls playing on the grass.

There were three of them from Luke's class at school, wearing shorts and cleats and kicking a soccer ball back and forth. One of them was new; she had come to school for the first time a few days ago. She looked serious about how she kicked that soccer ball. Luke wondered if he would ever kick a ball that well.

He'd hardly ever had a chance. Only a couple of times when their class played during P.E. on Wednesdays. There wasn't a regular P.E. coach, only their own teacher, Mrs. Schaffer, who usually had them do group games like Steal the Bacon or Dodgeball. A few times Paul Pickerell had brought his soccer ball to school and convinced Mrs. Schaffer to let them play. She didn't know how to referee, and the boys who played on the league teams always hogged the ball. Even the girls hated it and complained that they hardly ever got a chance to really play.

Out of the corner of his eye, Luke watched the three girls make a circle, but then Marcie Gurulé stopped the ball with her toe. "Hey, Luke, why aren't you playing with the Fighting Falcons? Aren't you on the team?"

Luke glanced sideways at her, avoiding the answer. Marcie was the prettiest girl in the sixth grade. Her waist-long black hair, streaked red from the sun, swung from side to side. Today, her fingernails matched her lavender sweatshirt and barrettes. She was one of the girls who fought for a chance to play during P.E. and complained the loudest. It was embarrassing to have the prettiest, most popular girl in class know he had never played a real game of soccer before.

Kasey Thompson, Marcie's best friend, shaded her eyes. "Are we going to play anymore?" she complained. "My mother wants me home by four-thirty."

Marcie threw her hair over one shoulder. "You're such a worrywart, Kasey. Hey, watch this!" She tapped the ball with her foot, popping it straight into the air. The soccer ball bounced off her knee and she caught it with both hands. Like an expert.

Luke watched Kasey throw up her skinny arms as if she was afraid the ball would hit her in the face.

"Kasey," Marcie said. "You can't be scared of the ball!" She turned to Luke again. "Why aren't you on the team? Don't you play?"

"Afraid to play with Paul, I bet," Kasey said, watching Luke out of the corner of her eye.

Marcie sighed. "I love to watch Paul play. He's *so* good. Don't you think so, Amelia?"

The new girl lifted her shoulders. "Maybe, but I'll bet I'm better than he is."

Marcie raised an eyebrow. "Think you're hot stuff?"

"Maybe, maybe not," Amelia said, mashing the grass with her own ball. "I can't believe this town doesn't have a girl's league. I've only been here a week and already I want to move."

"In the younger leagues, it's boys and girls mixed up together," Marcie told her. "But after you turn ten, the girl's league doesn't exist. The grown-ups say there isn't enough interest or coaches to go around."

"That's so unfair!" Amelia turned to Luke, pushing straggly yellow hair out of her eyes. "Hey, you want to kick the ball around with us?"

Luke shook his head. "I gotta go," he said as a way of saying good-bye. He wasn't going to let a hotshot like Paul see him playing with a bunch of girls. He glanced backward. The boys were in their positions for a new kickoff. Paul stood in the center, hunched over and ready to explode against the ball.

"Paul!" Coach Pickerell yelled. "Look alive! A second player has to touch the ball before you can take it down-field. Get it right this time."

Paul's face clenched. "Yes, sir," he muttered.

As Luke moved away, he heard Amelia murmur, "Tough coach."

Marcie nodded. "But he's always got the best team in town. I heard that Paul's older brother Phil made the college team. He might even get on one of the American League teams someday."

Luke's head jerked up. That was his dream, too. And the way to do it was to get on Coach Pickerell's team. Luke wanted to be on that team more than anything else. But there was no way. By the time he was old enough to get a job to pay for soccer fees and equipment, he'd be too old to learn.

He sprinted across the field and jumped onto the dusty ditch bank. A distant cheer rose like a dreamy echo behind him. Tomás Abeyta's team had scored their first point against Paul's team. In their jerseys, blue side out, the boys leapt with excitement, slapping hands in the air. There was a tie now.

Luke ignored the shouting voices and began to run, following the twisting path along the muddy ditch. The sun had dropped. It hung like an orange balloon above the towering bosque cottonwood forest. Yellow leaves rustled in the breeze, reminding Luke that autumn was in full swing. Soccer season was in full swing, too; still another month to go until the season ended.

And as always, Mr. Perea and Mama needed him.

Old Rex followed him at a slow trot, skin sagging, paws silent as Luke rounded a bend and jumped through knee-high prickly ragweed. A tumbleweed bumped down the path in the wind and Luke hurdled over it. He liked going home through the bosque with its magnificent, enormous cottonwoods. The bosque was a place to think and be by yourself. A place to kick a soccer ball if you had one.

He kicked at the dirt and found a rock under the swirling New Mexico dust. Pretending the rock was a soccer ball, he toed the stone, knocking it along the path until he reached the garbage dumpsters at the entrance to the trailer park.

An aging wooden sign swung silently in the breeze. Luke could barely make out the words *Rio Grande Trailer Park—A Home for Your Home*. Most of the letters had splintered and cracked.

"I'm only twenty-six," Mama had told Luke one day when he was nine. "I'm still young, and we have to get you to college someday. I hope," she had added, crossing herself and sending a glance heavenward. She was going to save their money, go to beauty school, get her license, and open her own shop. But the dream was still that. Just a dream. Like his own dream of being a soccer star.

The trailer park was deserted. Old Mrs. Garcia wasn't out sweeping her dirt front yard. Mr. Aragon wasn't walking his pet poodle, Curly. All the residents of the trailer park were inside their single-wide aluminum trailers fixing dinner or watching television.

Luke stopped at the three dented trash dumpsters. He and Anthony had scavenged dumpsters around town for a couple of years. That's how they found most of their stuff. Luke was lucky to get a couple of pairs of jeans and some T-shirts at the K-Mart sales in August before school started. Mama shopped at thrift stores, finding his winter jacket and half-worn shoes for cheap. Rent on the trailer and groceries took almost every bit of her restaurant wages. The little bit left over went into the bank account for beauty school someday.

Luke liked to think of himself as a forager instead of a scavenger. It sounded more important, dignified. A forager knew how to pick the best junk. Scavengers fought for the leftovers. Being a forager was his job. He couldn't get a paper route because the distances in their rural area were too great and he didn't have a bicycle, especially now that Anthony was gone. He had let Luke ride his old bike that was too small, but at least Luke had learned how to ride. Mowing lawns didn't work for a part-time job, either. Most yards were dirt and weeds.

"Remember the time Anthony and I found those great magazines," Luke told Rex as the dog lay down on the dirt road and put his head between his paws.

"*Popular Science* and *Car & Driver*. They had some good posters for my bedroom. Except the ones with applesauce spilled on them."

Old Rex raised his head and sniffed, as Luke peered over the edge to make sure there was a clear landing spot.

He backed up, got a running head start and scrambled up the side of the first brown, rusted dumpster. The container rumbled when Luke swung his legs over and hit the bottom. The blue sky seemed far away as he stood up and dusted off his jeans. The insides of the dumpster felt claustrophobic, like a cave.

There wasn't anything in this one today. A few brown bags leaked food. It stank bad and swarms of flies buzzed above the garbage. Luke climbed back out and tried the second big dumpster.

A corded stack of yellowed newspapers had been thrown into this bin and Luke took a seat on them. Two or three back issues of *Good Housekeeping* were stuck in a plastic bag in the corner. He set those aside for Mama.

A baby doll with a broken arm wasn't worth anything to him, but he took the miniature green army men next to it. Luke unwound the extension cord wrapped around a cracked lamp. He could take it home and see if it worked.

He piled his stuff in the corner, feeling pleased as he surveyed his haul. Actually, he was having a very good day.

Then, in the third and last dumpster, Luke uncovered his best find ever. Quickly, he pushed aside a soggy cardboard box and squished through a pile of rotting green slime. His heart began to pound under his T-shirt and he hardly dared to breathe. Were his eyes playing tricks?

Under a pile of grubby rags and broken, oozing jars of baby food, there lay a lost or abandoned blue-and-white soccer ball.

———————————

TWO

Luke kicked aside the broken bottles and tenderly picked up the soccer ball. He reached down for one of the grimy rags and wiped off a blotch of strained orange carrots.

The white part of the ball was dirty and the blue hexagons were badly scuffed. The ball was deflated, too. The sides were caved in, which reminded him of Mr. Perea, who often forgot to wear his fake teeth.

Mr. Perea! Luke sucked in his breath and glanced up. What time was it? Mama was probably on her way home and he hadn't started dinner or checked on their old neighbor yet.

Luke grabbed the women's magazines he'd laid aside for Mama, stuffed the army men into the same sack, then tucked the soccer ball under his shirt and hefted himself up to the rim of the dumpster.

He jumped down to the dirt, sneaking a glance down the street. He noticed that Old Rex had already gone home. Had anyone else seen him?

"Yoohoo! Hey!" a familiar voice hollered.

Heart sinking, Luke quickly folded his arms across the lump under his shirt.

On the corner of the unpaved street, Rosie Montoya hung out of her trailer door, a baby perched on her hip. The baby gummed a cracker, drooling all over its fist.

"Hey, Luke Espinosa!" Rosie called, raising a hand above her eyes to squint at him. "Where you going?"

Luke kicked up dust in the road. "Where do you think? I'm going to the moon."

Rosie snickered, letting him know she knew he was just joking. Luke figured she'd probably been lying on the couch in front of the TV all day.

Luke thought of her as the Soap Queen. Rosie watched soap operas all day long. Sometimes she stopped Luke on his way home from school, just to tell him the new story lines that week.

Rosie took another step in her tight, frayed jeans, holding the screen door open with one bare, brown foot. "I know where you been," she said, glancing up the road.

She *had* been spying on him. "So what!" he yelled, tired of her tricks.

"Your Mama home yet?"

"Nope." He walked on, keeping his back to her.

"Hey, Luke, your shirt looks funny. What you got hidden under there?"

"None of your business." Actually, he didn't dislike Rosie. She was just a pain. Always pestering and coming over.

"Hey, didn't your Mama tell you not to talk rude to a grown-up!" Rosie persisted.

"So grow up," Luke muttered, feeling mean. Coming

home to the trailer park always burst his daydreams at the soccer fields. Reality hit again and his envy toward Paul erupted. All those fancy soccer moves. Jealousy twisted Luke's heart into knots when he thought about Coach Pickerell and Paul playing soccer on their front lawn together. One day Paul would end up playing professional ball just like his brother. It was all there just waiting for him. He had the talent and the father to help him. Luke felt like he had nothing. He was just cursed with a longing that ached all the way to his toes.

Rosie shifted the baby, who whimpered to be let down, over to her other hip. "Tell your mama I want her to do my hair. Ramón's bringing home an extra half-gallon of ice cream from the dairy I'll give her for payment. Okay?"

Luke stopped. The ice cream got him, and she knew it. Mama could rarely afford treats, only for birthdays and holidays. "Okay. I'll tell her," he called back. A moment later he got an idea of his own and stopped again. "Hey, Rosie!"

She was still standing on her dinky little broken porch watching him.

"Do you have an air pump? Like for a bicycle?"

"A bicycle pump? No," she screeched back. "What you need one for? You ain't got a bike."

"Nothing." He wasn't about to tell her what for.

"Hey, Luke! Hey! Luke! Hey!" Rosie continued to scream, but he paid no attention and cut across the street. Luke banged the front door, shutting out Rosie's persistent shouts.

The small trailer living room was dim. Previous tenants had nailed up dark wooden panelling. Mama had placed two overstuffed, unmatched armchairs and a scratched coffee table in a circle. The table was littered with junk mail and old newspapers. A standing lamp hung over one of the chairs in the corner. The gray shade needed dusting.

Luke pulled at Mama's homemade curtains, letting in the late afternoon light and setting a thousand dust motes dancing. He plopped into the armchair, stuck the plastic bag on the floor, and pulled out his new-found treasure.

It was real. A genuine, leather soccer ball. His very own. After years of dreaming and wishing, it was almost too much to believe.

He'd never told his mother. She'd want to pull her hard-earned money out of the sacred bank account and sign him up for soccer. Signing up meant money for the fee, money for a ball, money for shorts and the reversible jerseys, shin guards, the extra long socks, and new shoes so he wouldn't slip on the grass fields during games. Soccer meant cash.

But now he had a ball. He always thought that if he only had a chance he could be as good as Paul and Tomás. Perhaps even better.

Lovingly he touched the worn leather and tried to pull out the creases. It didn't work. He needed a pump. But what if the ball had a hole or a leak and was impossible to fill?

In the kitchen, Luke turned on the faucet and washed off the carrot stains with cleanser. When he dried the leather with a towel the blue hexagons stuck out bright and bold. The best soccer ball he'd ever seen. And it was his.

The clock on the stove reminded Luke once more of the vanishing afternoon. He'd promised Mama he'd start dinner for her. Luke jogged down the narrow hallway to his bedroom, flipped the pillow over and stuck the lopsided ball underneath.

Back in the kitchen he started a pot of brown beans simmering. Then he hurriedly measured a cup of rice into a pan of water, spilling grains on the floor. From the refrigerator, he pulled out a package of flour tortillas, slopped margarine on several, and stuck them in the oven to warm.

Now it was time for Mr. Perea. Luke ran to the neighboring trailer, knocking loudly so Eduardo Perea could hear him. He heard a croaky, deep voice and stepped into a tiny, cramped living room.

From under the porch, Rex got up, climbed the steps, and pushed his way past Luke's legs. The dog plopped himself down in front of the sofa where Mr. Perea was lying under a purple-and-green afghan, his boots hanging out one end.

Half-eaten bowls of chicken soup and bottles of Mr. Perea's heart medication sat on the table. Dust lay thick as chimney soot on top of the bookcases. Smells of cough syrup hung in the air. Luke wished Mr. Perea would open the windows, but a portable heater rattled loudly in the corner, its burning wire rods looking like cherry-red licorice ropes.

The television was turned up even louder than the heater. Mr. Perea motioned Luke over with an ancient, gnarled hand. "Come, *mi hijo*," he said in a thick accent. "You not been around in days." He grinned and coughed, obviously pleased to see Luke.

Luke sat on the edge of an armchair, trying to be patient. "I was here yesterday. I come most days, except when Mama has her days off."

Eduardo Perea chuckled. "How could I miss you?" He pulled the blanket closer. "It is cold, no? Winter is coming. Eighty-five this year and my old bones will not take it."

Luke covered the man's hand with his own, checking for fever. He was warm, but not hot. Mr. Perea's skin felt dry and paper thin, covered with blue, mottled veins and dark brown age spots. Old people felt a little weird, he thought. Luke got up to collect the food dishes strewn about the room. "Did you take your medicine?"

Mr. Perea's bony face bobbed up and down. "*Sí, sí,* I remember that, but the cough does not leave."

Luke took the pile of dishes into the kitchen and stuck them in the sink. "What do you want for dinner, Mr. Perea?"

There wasn't any answer. Luke walked back into the living room. The old man wasn't paying any attention. The commercials were over and his program had returned. He leaned over excitedly, trying to sit up, but his black boots tangled in the afghan. "*Sí, sí,*" he whispered in a raspy quiver. "That is the way with the ball. Careful! Drive to the forward—back again. Watch the other man! Aargh! Foul!"

Luke fell into the armchair. This was the one good thing about helping Mr. Perea. He had cable and loved to watch the soccer games.

Mr. Perea slapped his thigh and his eyes gleamed like two black marbles. "Today *es España.*" The elderly man leaned over and his breath smelled like burnt coffee and stale cigarette smoke. "You boy, you are lucky. You are young, *qué no?* I warn you. Do not give up your life for soccer. Go to college. Get a job."

It was hard for Luke to imagine Mr. Perea, the cranky, coughing old buzzard as a soccer player. He had played on an amateur team in Mexico sixty years ago. "Playing soccer is not a big thing. Look where I end up. Dumpy house, no flower garden. Aah, Maria's flowers. They are beautiful." His tone shifted and the old man started mumbling about his dead wife and her old rose gardens in the city, plucking at a loose purple thread in the blanket.

Luke turned the volume down. Half a minute left. Spain was ahead of Portugal by three, so the outcome seemed easy to predict.

In the gloomy kitchen, Luke turned on the overhead light. The bulb sparked and went out. Luke rummaged through the cupboards until he found a new one. He dumped the dead bugs out of the fixture, then fastened it back into the ceiling. He heated a can of mushroom soup and mixed a pitcher of grape Kool-aid, then buttered a piece of toast and took the meal out to the old man, who was now watching the Telemundo News in Spanish.

"I'll be back tomorrow," he told Mr. Perea.

Eduardo Perea nodded. "You come back *mañana.* Bring me a Coke. I could drink a Coke."

Old Rex stirred on the floor. The animal was so quiet Luke had forgotten him. He filled a bowl with dog food and freshened the water bowl in the kitchen. At the front door Luke said, "Uh, Mr. Perea? You wouldn't happen to have an air pump would you, like for tires?"

The old man slurped his Kool-aid and waved Luke away. *"No sé.* Maybe the shed. *Mañana*—I want to watch the weather."

⚽ THREE

At home, the soccer ball was still stashed under his pillow, deflated, but beautiful. Luke wished it was tomorrow so he could look for an air pump in Mr. Perea's shed. *No holes*, he thought. The ball had to be all right. In a few weeks he would stroll onto the soccer fields and punt and pop the ball around like a superstar. Everybody would be in awe. They would beg him to be on their team, pay his way, buy him a uniform.

What a dream. But it would work. Luke knew it could. Because he had a plan. He was so caught up in his daydream, he didn't hear Mama open the door.

"Hello, *hijo*," she said, kissing the top of his hair. She kicked off her shoes and sank into an armchair. "Smells good, Luke."

"Just beans and tortillas."

Cristina Espinosa unpinned the tight knot of hair at the back of her neck. Her brown eyes looked big in her small face. "I think I'm so tired I'm not even hungry. I hate the six A.M. breakfast shifts. I don't know which shift is worse—days or nights."

On Saturdays, Luke walked downtown to the post office to pick up their mail and visit his mother at Harry's and get a soda. Usually Mama spent the whole time running back and forth. To the kitchen for orders, back to the counter, filling water glasses, ringing up bills on the cash register. Big, burly truckers pulled in, driving enormous semis. They ordered fast, ate fast, and slapped their tips on the counter.

"You'll feel better after supper," Luke told her, smiling. He couldn't help it. He was so close to having his very own soccer ball. Even the beans looked good, though they ate them five or six times a week.

Mama untied the work apron and left it on the counter. The rice was only a little burnt, but Luke didn't think she noticed.

"You seem happy, baby," she observed. "School is good, yes?"

Luke shrugged, trying to be patient. He wanted to surprise her with his soccer talent in a few weeks.

"Did you go see Mr. Perea?"

"Yeah, he's fine. Oh, Rosie wants you to do her hair."

Mama sighed and closed her eyes.

"She said she's got ice cream," Luke added.

Mama ate a spoonful of beans and smiled. "Then I'll do it for you and the ice cream. Rosie is funny, *verdad?* I think she's lonely. Got married and had a baby too young." Mama laughed at herself. "I should talk—I was younger when I gave birth to you."

When they finished eating, Mama changed out of the waitress uniform and got into her pink bathrobe. She put her feet up on the coffee table, clearing the mail. In the evenings, she worked on her fingernails while she sang along to the country western station. "I don't want dishwater ugly hands," she always said. Besides, she was in training for when she went to beauty school. The cheap manicure set lay in a neat array across the coffee table. Files and miniature scissors and emery boards. Bottles of polish ranged in rows from light pink to deep red.

"Get my purse, would you, Luke?" she asked, frowning at her hands.

He got up from the table where he was trying to figure out his math homework. The handbag sat on the cramped counter top, perched between the dish drainer and the toaster. When Luke reached, it fell to the floor.

The clasp had broken and the contents spilled out in a tumble. Lipstick, wallet, keys, old grocery receipts. And a snapshot. A faded photograph of his mother standing in front of a high school football stadium with a man. Mama was a teenager, wearing tight jeans and a fluffy, red blouse. Her dark hair blew in an invisible breeze. The man had his arm around her neck, pulling her to him and smiling. One finger touched the tip of a long-handled mustache.

When Luke was younger there had been other pictures. He tried to remember, but it was so long ago. Pictures in frames on Mama's bedside table. Over time, the pictures disappeared. But he knew the man was his father and the old snapshot socked him right in the gut.

Questions he hadn't thought about in years shot like bullets through his mind. Why was a picture suddenly in Mama's purse? Did she think about him? Did she miss him? His mother hadn't mentioned his father's name in years, and Luke hadn't asked since he was a little kid. There was no reason. His father was someone he'd never met, never talked to, and knew nothing about. But he'd been thinking about fathers a lot lately. Deep inside, Luke wanted to know what had happened to him. But it was hard to ask when Mama never wanted to talk about it.

"Thanks, baby," she said, reaching for the purse. She stopped, seeing the photo in his hands.

He looked at her, his muscles taut as a spring. "Have you heard from him?"

She took the picture from his fingers, shaking her head. "I haven't seen him since you were two years old. You know that. Were you hoping for something?"

Luke balled a dish towel and pitched it into the kitchen, but the cloth hit the cupboard and fell to the floor. He shrugged, but his jaw quivered. "I don't care."

Mama set down the emery board and rubbed her fingers across her leg. "So many years. At first he sent money, but—" Her lips tightened.

"Do you ever want to see him again?" Luke asked. "Are you sorry he's gone?"

Mama smiled wearily. "You know this already, *hijo*. I used to be terribly sorry. I used to pray on my knees that he would help me. I went to mass every day, talked to the priests. I hoped he would send money for you. But he never did. I didn't graduate high school, but we've done good, haven't we?" She held out her hand. "Haven't we, baby?"

"Why are you carrying his picture?"

"I—sometimes—" she broke off. "I get scared—oh, it's just silly . . ."

Luke watched her face, and the nervous feeling came charging back. "Are you trying to find him?"

She picked up a bottle of pink polish, hitting it against her palm. "No, I'm sure he won't help us. He's probably a drunk bum somewhere."

But she said this last statement as though she didn't really believe it.

Luke went back to the table and stared at the rows of decimal problems smeared across the paper. Finding the picture of his father made him want to crumple up the homework and throw it across the kitchen just like the dish towel. Even math seemed harder without Anthony, who always knew how to figure out the hard stuff.

The trailer felt cramped and dreary now. All because of somebody he didn't even know, and had never met. It was strange how fast this good day of finding his own soccer ball had turned sour.

⚽ FOUR

Mama had the six o'clock breakfast shift again. Luke ate a bowl of cornflakes and fixed a peanut butter sandwich to take for lunch.

He liked Fridays because Mrs. Schaffer did art. Big projects like papier-mâché piñatas and murals painted on rolls of butcher paper along the classroom walls. This month they were making a quilt. Everybody was going to make two squares. One square was supposed to depict something they liked—a talent or a hobby. The other square was to be their favorite scene or character from the book Mrs. Schaffer had finished reading aloud.

When all the squares were done, Mrs. Schaffer was going to sew them into a huge blanket. Then she would hang it in the classroom for the rest of the year. "I have ten quilts at home from all my sixth-grade classes," she had told them. "That way I can remember all my students."

Luke pulled out a piece of blank paper and started drawing the design he wanted for his personal square. He watched the rest of the class break up into small groups to work together. Mrs. Schaffer let the class talk or work in groups—if they didn't get too wild.

Marcie sat two desks in front of Luke. Jeff, the boy who sat directly behind her, was absent today so Luke could see what she had chosen for her project. Marcie was lining up piles of colored thread on her desk in neat, perfect rows. Reds, greens, yellows, blues, and purples. On a piece of cloth she had drawn the figure of a movie actress and was going to embroider it using all the colored threads.

Kasey shoved her desk over and lined it side by side with Marcie's. She was copying Marcie's idea, except she had chosen a different actress.

Luke watched them whispering and giggling as the new girl sauntered down the aisle, holding a handful of squeezable paint tubes. Luke tried to remember her name, but couldn't.

The girl stopped at Marcie's desk. "Oh yuck! Embroidery? Didn't they do that in the Middle Ages?"

Marcie tossed her head and long, dark hair came flying back toward Luke. "Embroidery takes a lot of skill."

The girl raised an eyebrow. "You can do that using paint. Mrs. Schaffer's got about twenty different colors. And it's a lot easier."

"Thanks anyway," Marcie replied. "Everybody else is using those tube paints. We want our squares to look unique, don't we Kasey?"

Kasey nodded like a puppet.

The girl leaned over Marcie's desk, peering through her straggly bangs. "Hey, we playing soccer this afternoon?"

Luke watched the girls over the top of his desk.

"Maybe," Marcie said. "If it's not too hot."

"It's not hot," the girl said. "It's October." She glanced at Luke. "You want to play, too?"

Startled, Luke shook his head. He wouldn't play with the Falcons watching. No way.

"Don't you love this color?" Marcie said, holding up a length of hot pink strands. "I think I'll make her dress out of this. A low cut dress with sequins."

Kasey giggled and snapped her embroidery hoop together, accidentally knocking over the package of needles.

Across the aisle Paul Pickerell laughed. "Hey, watch where you're throwing those weapons!"

Kasey reached down to pick up the needles as Marcie pretended to throw one at Paul. "Catch this, Falcon!"

Luke tried to ignore the horseplay—it bugged him to see Paul get so much attention all the time. He studied his drawing. It was turning out well. A soccer player leapt high in the air, legs bent, muscles rippling, sweaty hair flying. His athlete had just tipped the ball with his toe and sent it whamming into the goal box. Luke added hexagons to the ball and shaded them in.

Suddenly someone was breathing down his neck.

Luke stuck his arm over his paper.

"Too late, Espinosa," Paul muttered in his ear. "I saw it. You stole my idea."

Luke flipped the sheet over and looked into Paul's face. The boy's pale blue eyes unnerved Luke. The classroom suddenly felt as hot as an August afternoon.

"I didn't steal nothing," Luke said.

"Yes, you did," Paul insisted, grabbing a paper off

his own desk. "See, my picture's finished and you just started."

With dismay, Luke saw that Paul had also drawn a sketch of a soccer player. The player had just bounced a ball off his forehead, but it looked like he was dangling in the air. There wasn't any background drawn in.

"I guess you thought I had a good idea and wanted to copy it," Paul said. "But it would look dumb to have two soccer pictures on the quilt. And *you* don't even play."

"You don't know everything, Pickerell," Luke said. He wasn't giving in. His picture was better than Paul's, and he wanted it on that class quilt.

"Oh, really? What is it I don't know, Espino*so*? I got the Most Valuable Player award at the banquet last year."

Luke couldn't stop the rising jealousy in the pit of his stomach. He didn't bother to correct Paul's mispronunciation of his name, either. It wouldn't do any good anyway. He sat stiffly, willing the other boy to leave.

Mrs. Schaffer looked up from her desk. "Talk quietly, please. This is a privilege."

Glancing at the teacher, Paul lowered his voice a notch. "I'm going to be a professional soccer player someday just like my brother. You'll be able to watch me on television." He leaned across Luke's desk and hissed, "Check this out—camera close-ups, instant replays. Just watch where you drool," he added, snickering.

Luke sucked in his breath. It was strange to hear his own dream coming out of Paul Pickerell's mouth.

"Hey, on Sunday there are tournament tryouts, Espinoso. I've made tournament team the last three years. Why don't you come?"

"You mean try out too?" Luke's voice practically squeaked.

"No, you dope." Paul laughed. "You have to be on one of the regular teams and play the season. But you can watch the rest of us. I guarantee it'll make your weekend more exciting."

"I don't know. I got stuff to do."

"What kind of stuff?"

Luke shrugged. "Just things."

Paul shook his head. "You're strange, Espinoso. But take my advice. Try another picture. This one ain't gonna cut it."

Mrs. Schaffer adjusted her glasses. "Mr. Pickerell, do I need to warn you again?"

"It's not my fault," Paul whined innocently. "Luke drew the same picture I did. Look!" He seized both drawings and held them up.

Luke grabbed for his, but snatched at thin air. His face burned. He didn't want anybody to see the picture until it was finished.

Paul turned to let the classroom view the drawings.

"Luke doesn't even play soccer," Paul said. "I'm the Falcon captain and we're undefeated this season."

Mrs. Schaffer took off her glasses. "Well, that's very nice, Paul, but obviously Luke has an interest in soccer, too. I don't think anybody would mind if we had two soccer squares on the quilt."

"It would look dumb," Mike Burrell shot across the room. He was Paul's best friend and also on the Falcon team.

Luke stared at his desk, wishing everybody would just shut up. From the corner of his eye he saw the new girl jumping up and down in her seat, her arm raised high like a flag, fingers wiggling. Mrs. Schaffer didn't call on her but suddenly she burst out, "You could put the squares on two different ends of the quilt."

"That's a good idea—" the teacher began.

"Or we could take a vote," the girl added, "I vote for Luke's picture. His soccer player looks like he's going to jump off the page and start scoring right here in our classroom."

"Good observation, Amelia," Mrs. Schaffer noted. "But I think both boys can have their pictures on the quilt."

"Hey, Marcie," Paul shouted, not to be outdone. "Which picture do you think is better?"

Luke stiffened as the entire classroom started talking now, taking sides. Marcie stared at the drawings and licked her lips. "I don't have to vote if I don't want to," she said finally.

Mrs. Schaffer looked grateful. "I agree with Marcie. There's no need to vote. Now everybody back to work. It's almost lunchtime."

Just then a group of students painting in the corner by the sink spilled a bottle of green paint. It oozed down the cabinets and Mrs. Schaffer jumped up, grabbing a roll of paper towels.

Paul leaned over and slammed Luke's drawing down on the desk, crumpling the corner he was holding. "You're getting on my nerves, Espinoso."

⚽ FIVE

When the afternoon bell rang, Luke skipped soccer practice and raced down the ditch banks, anxious to get to Mr. Perea's. He'd brought some change from his bottom dresser drawer and stopped at the grocery store to buy an RC Cola for the old man. He pulled one off a six-pack because they were cheaper than the drinks in the refrigerated section.

Eduardo Perea grinned when he saw the soda. "We split it. To celebrate Mexico's victory in the World Cup."

"But the World Cup isn't until next summer," Luke said, pulling two plastic cups from the cupboard.

Mr. Perea tapped his forehead. "I think positive." He laughed hoarsely and snapped the tab on the can.

The old man looked better today. He clumped around the kitchen, snapping his suspenders over his baggy black pants, and broke ice into the glasses. Luke poured the soda, making sure the cups were even.

"I know a famous soccer player once," Mr. Perea said, smacking his lips. "He live next door. I went to university—watch his games. When he play they always win. He make a punt over his head that is *beautiful*. Right in the net. That net is like a big open mouth waiting for a piece of chocolate."

Luke smiled. These were the old man's favorite stories. About a soccer player he'd known probably fifty years ago. Luke suspected Mr. Perea had been jealous of him. He'd gone on to play professionally in Mexico, and Eduardo Perea had come to the U.S., but was only able to play on amateur teams. That was one of the reasons that Mr. Perea was always telling him to forget about soccer and go to college. But now there was the American Soccer League with professional teams in over a dozen cities.

Mr. Perea eyed him as if he knew what Luke was thinking. "But you. *You* get a job in a bank."

Luke eyed him right back. "I'm going to be a famous soccer player, same as him. And you can tell everyone you lived next door to me, too."

The old man laughed and slapped Luke on the shoulder. "I will be passed out of this life before you finish into a man, boy," he said. "You are *loco*. Crazy, *loco*. And now, you are about to jump from your shoes, boy. What do you need?"

"You said you might have a bicycle pump I could borrow."

Mr. Perea rapped his fist against the kitchen counter. "*Sí, sí.* Out in the shed."

Luke followed him across the dirt yard to the back of the lot. Mr. Perea fussed with the padlock a moment and then the shed doors creaked open. Dim, dusty light filtered through the cracks in the roof and a stale smell poured out into the October afternoon.

A soft, padding sound rustled behind them and Old Rex lumbered toward them, panting. Luke held out his hand and the dog nudged his wet nose into his palm. Mr. Perea pointed toward a hefty rock and Luke rolled it against the door to anchor it. Old Rex lay down in the shade of a bush to watch.

"Good boy," Mr. Perea said to his dog as Luke followed him into the shed. He felt a huge stab of dismay. The shed was eight feet wide and eight feet long and looked crammed with fifty years' worth of flea market merchandise. A dented refrigerator faced the wall next to a sofa whose three round springs stuck straight out of the cushions. Dozens of stacked boxes were heaped everywhere, contents spilling out. A torn shower curtain, green with mildew, hung over a nail in the wall.

As they stood staring at the shed's mess, Mr. Perea sighed and scratched his stomach. "I remember a pump," he murmured. "Somewhere in here."

Luke spied a couple of bicycles in the far corner. They were definitely old, with wide, bumpy tires and splintered metal frames, but it gave him hope.

They began to dig.

A quick glance showed it wasn't lying on the floor or in between the sofa springs, so they divided the shed in half and started on the boxes. After fifteen minutes Luke was covered in grime and Mr. Perea had started to wheeze. Luke licked his lips and his teeth felt gritty. He rubbed his mouth with the back of his sleeve and wondered if a bicycle pump really existed. Or if it was only in Mr. Perea's memory.

Then Luke saw a two-foot-wide shelf running high along the back of the shed. It was piled with boxes, too.

The old man nodded. "We try the shelves. Go to the house and get a chair."

Luke ran back to Mr. Perea's trailer and hauled one of the kitchen chairs across the yard. Grunting, Mr. Perea shoved several boxes to the side, clearing a space on the floor.

Luke hopped on the chair and strained to see the dim recesses of the dark shelf. Fortunately, there were only a few boxes. With his fingertips, Luke shook each box to figure out what was inside. Several of the solid, heavy boxes were filled with books. Two more held figurines and ceramics wrapped in old newspaper.

"Maria's," Mr. Perea said, referring to his deceased wife.

Luke scooted the chair farther down and climbed up again. From out of the shadows he made out a long, smooth cylinder sticking out of the back of a box.

"I think I found it," he said, hope surging.

Mr. Perea peered up at him. "Can you lift the box down?"

"I think so." Luke shook the box. It was taller and a little wider than the others, but it didn't feel very heavy. He slid the box across the shelf toward him inch by inch, wishing the chair was taller because it was hard to get a good grip. After a minute his arms were tingling like crazy, but now it was too late to stop and rest. The carton was coming down whether he was ready or not.

Luke fumbled, trying to grab the corners better, but suddenly the chair legs tilted on the uneven floor and the box slipped. Luke knew he couldn't save it. Instinctively he covered his head as the box gave a jerk and flipped over.

Soccer balls began raining down on top of him.

SIX

One of the balls hit Luke on the head and ricocheted off the corner of the refrigerator. Two bounced off the couch in opposite directions and another landed on the floor with a thud. Mr. Perea caught the fifth in his hands, and began to laugh in his raspy voice.

"I forgot about that box," he said, shaking his head.

Luke righted the tipped chair and began to retrieve the balls. Even though there were only five soccer balls it felt like fifty when they were falling on top of him. But they were as flat as his own ball, hidden under the pillow at home. He bent over and picked up the bicycle pump that had also toppled out. A bundle of old tire tubes and a metal wheel rim clattered to the floor.

"I look for these," Mr. Perea said, holding the metal rim in his hands. "To fix my bike."

"I could have helped you," Luke said. He had a hard time imagining Mr. Perea riding a bike.

Mr. Perea laughed. "I think I look for them before you were born. And my balls! Aye! I forget they are here. I had a plan to fix them, but see, they are punctured."

Luke picked up one of the balls, turning it over. The leather was hard and brittle. The balls were so ancient, the skin of each one looked scaly, like a fish.

Mr. Perea seemed to read his mind. "My first soccer ball," he said, pointing to the one Luke held. "When I am twelve. These balls I buy later, when I play for the leagues. Sixty years ago. *Dios mío.* My mind is hard to believe this."

"Do you want me to put them back in the box for you?" Luke asked.

Mr. Perea stroked the balls, picking at the leather with his finger. Stiff little pieces broke off. He shook his head. "No, I take the balls inside. Help me."

Luke picked up three of the balls and the pump. He stuck the tire rims and tubes back in the box, then shut the shed doors.

Dusk was falling and Luke switched on the living room lamp.

"Cold, no?" Mr. Perea grunted. He fell into a chair and pulled the afghan over him. "Turn on the weather," he instructed.

"No soccer today?"

The old man shook his head. "No soccer game. Just soccer balls. Take the pump and go, boy," he said abruptly. "I see you tomorrow."

"Are you okay?" Luke asked.

"*Sí, sí,*" he said impatiently. "Just remember, boy," he added, his black marble eyes piercing the gloomy trailer. "Don't dream too much. Dreams can hurt." Then Mr. Perea waved him away.

As Luke went out the front door, he glanced back, the old man's sadness tugging at him, but he didn't know what to say. Mr. Perea had piled the five old soccer balls from the past in his lap. He was examining each of them intently, rubbing his crooked fingers over the rigid leather folds. The old man's gray, weathered face had fallen into quiet, sagging folds.

Luke slowly walked back home, thinking about Mr. Perea's words, but as soon as he was through the front door of his own trailer he ran to his bedroom and grabbed the blue-and-white ball from under the pillow. He stuck the needle into the ball, holding the pump steady with his foot while he pushed down with both hands. The ball made a funny slurping sound after being flattened so long. The next few hours were the test. The ball had to last through the night without losing air.

When he went to bed, Luke stared at the ball next to his pillow until his eyes burned. When he woke up the next morning, the first thing he saw, lying two inches from his nose, was the soccer ball. And it held! The ball was still round and firm.

Lying on the bed in his pajamas, Luke popped the ball between his hands, loving the curved, smooth feel of the leather. He flicked it into the air and caught it over and over again. But he couldn't play just yet. It was time to put his plan in motion.

Luke stuck his legs into his jeans and threw a sweatshirt over his head. In the kitchen he hurriedly ate a bowl of cereal, leaving the empty dish on top of the growing pile in the sink.

The biggest job was going to be getting rid of his bed.

Luke stripped the bedding and piled the sheets in the corner. The single bed only had one mattress and he propped it against the living room wall. He'd take it out to the storage shed later. He hoped there was room. He couldn't remember how long it had been since he'd been inside the shed. They rarely went out there. Only when Mama needed her winter clothes. All he remembered were empty packing boxes and suitcases. The suitcases hadn't been used since they went to visit Mama's sister in California three years ago, and they didn't have a lawn mower or a car that needed tools and oil changing supplies. But that meant there should be plenty of room.

With the mattress off, Luke unscrewed the bolts holding the bed frame together. He lugged out the boards and slats and laid them in the hall beside the mattress.

Next he pushed the tall wooden dresser across the bedroom floor into the closet. He had to get on his knees to drive it over the puckered, worn carpet, but it fit okay. Then he dug into the bottom drawer and pulled out the hammock he had been saving. Last summer he and Anthony had found the hammock in a dumpster near a fancy neighborhood across town. They never had a chance to try it out before Anthony moved. With a blanket, the hammock would be as comfortable as a bed. And using a hammock would keep the floor space clear for practice.

Standing in the doorway, Luke surveyed his bedroom with all that empty, new space. It was great. It was perfect.

He searched through the stuff in his drawer again, picking out the screw-hooks he had found in the school dumpster last month. He got a chair to stand on, but realized he had better wait to pound the holes for the screws. Mama loved her mornings off for sleeping late.

Taking the old, dusty hammock into the kitchen, Luke filled the sink with hot water and poured in a scoop of laundry soap. When he sunk the hammock into the suds the water turned black. Luke had to refill the sink and start over again.

After it was rinsed, the soggy hammock weighed a ton. Luke lugged it outside and spread it over the railing of the porch to dry.

Back in his room, he grabbed the scuffed soccer ball. In stocking feet he toed the ball gently with the side of his foot, but the ball wasn't as easy to maneuver as he had thought. It didn't always go in the direction he wanted. Trying to move the ball with the insides of his feet, he lost his balance and hit the wall with his shoulder. Starting back across the room the second time, he went too fast and the ball ricocheted into the closet. Now his toes hurt.

Mama's bedroom door opened and the hall shower swished on. Luke hid his ball in the closet and went into the kitchen, pulling out the frying pan. He cracked three eggs and stirred them in the skillet. A few minutes later Mama came into the kitchen, her dark hair pulled back into one long, wet braid. She rolled the cooked eggs into warm tortillas and topped them with green chili and the leftover cheese from supper. "You ought to be out with other boys playing football or basketball or whatever it is they play around here," she said.

"Soccer." The word popped out before he could stop it.

"What?" Mama set down the plate of tortillas with a clatter.

"Soccer. That's what they play around here," Luke told her. It was impossible to keep it inside.

"Soccer?" Mama echoed and made the sign of the cross over her forehead and chest. *"Dios mío,"* she said in a funny voice. "I should have known."

"Known what?" Luke asked, feeling a pang in his stomach.

Mama looked away, her mouth a tight line. She began to pick at her red fingernails. "You don't want to play soccer, do you?"

Luke tried to act careless. "Most kids have been playing since they were little. I know we can't afford it."

Mama picked up her tortilla. She seemed relieved. "You're right. It would be too hard to start now that you're twelve." Suddenly she twisted her head, peering beyond the kitchen. "Why is your bed in the living room?"

Luke was prepared. "I found this great hammock and I want to sleep in it for awhile."

"I slept on a hammock once in—" she switched her sentence. *"Mi hijo,* it won't be comfortable. You won't sleep good."

"I think it'll be fun. I can swing in it and dangle my legs over the side."

"It's probably dirty. Let me wash it for you."

"I already did," Luke said.

His mother laughed. "I'll bet there's not another boy at school who does cooking and washing like you do."

That thought didn't exactly thrill him. None of the kids at school knew what a housewife he was. Her laughter angered him. He jumped up from the table and slammed the frying pan into the sink. "Don't think I like it!"

"You don't have to break the pan," Mama said. She got up and kissed him near his ear. "Where is your bed going?"

"In the storage shed."

"I suppose the shed is the best place," she said. "But it's locked. I'll have to find the key. Tomorrow morning I'll take it out there."

"I can do it. I'll be here all day."

Mama shook her head. "No, don't bother, I'll do it."

"But Mama . . ." He suddenly stopped. For some reason she didn't want him going out to the storage shed. But, why? There wasn't anything out there.

Mama tightened the cord on her bathrobe and disappeared into the bathroom.

Recalling the last time he had been inside the shed was impossible, but it seemed like whenever they went out there Mama was always with him. He couldn't remember ever going alone.

Luke narrowed his eyes, thinking. Maybe his mother made sure he didn't go looking for things she didn't want him to see. Luke laughed at himself. Now his imagination was getting crazy. She probably didn't want him messing things up. Mama was particular about things being boxed and orderly. Still, his curiosity began to grow even as he tried to shake it off.

The next couple of hours dragged by and he filled them with waiting. Waiting for the hammock to dry.

Waiting for Mama to leave.

Waiting to find the key to the storage shed.

Mama washed the dishes from breakfast, then mixed a bowl of flour, salt, and lard for a new batch of tortillas. Every Saturday morning she fried several stacks of fresh tortillas. Afterward, they ate hot ones for lunch with butter and beans. The rest went into plastic bags in the refrigerator for the next week's meals.

Luke tried to finish the math he hadn't done yesterday, but none of it made sense. He kept staring out the side window at the shed.

Mama finished mixing the dough. "Help me finish these tortillas, Luke."

They stood at the counter together and Luke squeezed off the dough into little balls while Mama expertly patted it between the palms of her hands until it stretched into a thin, round circle. A skillet greased with lard sat heating on the hot stove. Luke took the tortillas and cooked them in the pan for thirty seconds, baking them on both sides. He laid them on the steaming stack.

Making tortillas on Saturday was a tradition, and Luke couldn't wait to smother one with butter and cram it into his mouth. They were the best when they were fresh made.

Mama always said, "We have to wait until they're all finished. If we stop to eat, the oil will get too hot. Then we'll get too full in our stomachs to want to finish our work."

When they were finally done, Luke sat at the table and ate four in a row, while Mama packaged up several dozen in plastic bags. She wrapped another half-dozen tortillas in a clean kitchen towel for Mr. Perea. "I'll cut Rosie's hair after I finish fixing lunch for Mr. Perea," she said. "Then I'm working the dinner shift." Which meant three P.M. to midnight. And Mama usually didn't get home until after one in the morning because the cash register had to be closed out for the day.

While Mama was gone, Luke took the chance to twist the two screw-hooks into the ceiling. His fingers felt raw when he finished, but the hooks held tight. The hammock was dry, except for the tassel fringe. He strung it up on the hooks and tied the ends with knots. Luke tugged at it, testing his weight. Better to crash now than later, in the middle of the night.

Mama returned from Rosie's after Luke finished hanging up the hammock. While she got ready for work, Luke scuffed around outside, staring at the shed. The metal structure seemed to beckon him. Why didn't Mama want him in there? He couldn't figure out what sort of secret it might hold. It was bugging him.

Mama burst through the front door onto the porch steps, wearing a clean uniform. "The ice cream's in the freezer," she called. "Be good." On weekends Luke usually missed her a lot, but now he had his soccer ball. And he had work to do.

He felt like a real sneak looking through Mama's stuff, but he'd already looked through the stuff on the coffee table and rummaged through all the drawers in the kitchen.

The key had to be in her bedroom.

⚽ SEVEN

The shades were closed. Clothes lay strewn on the rumpled bed. Bottles of makeup, combs, and hairbrushes cluttered the top of the dresser. A cracked mirror hung on the wall and a pile of thumbed and worn paperback novels sat stacked on the floor. Mama bought them at a used bookstore for a dime each. After she read the pile she exchanged them for another.

Luke had never looked at his mother's room quite like this before. A place where things were hidden and waiting to be found.

After fifteen minutes of careful searching so as not to leave any telltale sign that he'd been in there, Luke felt like a dope when he found a silver, metallic key sitting in the bathroom drawer next to Mama's toothbrush. Eagerly, he clutched the key in his hand and headed for the door. That's when he saw the little brown book lying on the floor. He must have knocked it off the dresser when he was searching.

The word *Addresses* was stamped in black letters on the cover. Mama claimed she didn't know where his father was. At least, that's how she made it sound. He'd never been sure that was really true. Luke swallowed, knowing he had to look. He had to find out if his father was in the book.

Palms sweating, Luke perched on the edge of the bed and flipped the pages. A couple of the waitresses from Harry's restaurant were listed and a few old friends from California.

Luke paused, fingering the tabs with the letters *A* through *Z* on them. Slowly, he turned to the *E* page. Only one name was written down. Luke's stomach lurched clear into his throat. The last name was the same as his own. Espinosa. Ricardo Espinosa. Scribbled under Ricardo Espinosa's name was an address—1011 Calle de Piedra, Mexico Distrito Federal, Mexico. That was Mexico City.

Long-ago pictures were one thing. But an address was real. Attached to a real person. His father lived in a house, went to work, ate, played, everything.

Before he could think, Luke grabbed a scrap of paper, scribbled the address, and stuffed it into his jeans. He left the little book on the dresser, his heart pounding like a jackhammer.

The ridges of the key dug into his hand, reminding him of the job that lay ahead.

He was the forager at work now.

The shed doors creaked softly. It was pitch black inside and he stood waiting for his eyes to adjust. The shed wasn't anything like Mr. Perea's. Mama wasn't a packrat, and she hadn't had as many years to collect.

A broken ironing board leaned against a wall. Stacks of boxes filled with old clothes sat in their own mountainous pile. Mama had marked them with a pen: Luke—sizes 5, 6, 7.

An old green chair, the seat split and torn, stood next to them. Luke had forgotten about that chair. Without a car they couldn't take it to the dump. Carrying the chair in for Mama must have been the last time he was in the shed, about a year ago. Mama had unlocked it, Luke stuck the chair in, and she locked the place back up. The shed was a pretty empty, boring place. He'd never had a reason to go out here on his own before. Until now.

It must be his imagination that Mama was trying to keep him from coming out here. It was just a crummy old shed. Plenty of room for the bed frame and mattress.

He ran back across the yard and propped open the front door. Piece by piece he hauled out the bed frame. Dragging the mattress was much more difficult. The stupid thing kept buckling and folding over on itself, but Luke finally got it across the yard and threw it over the bed frame.

As he dusted his hands on his jeans, a glitter of metal deep in the back corner caught a thin ray of sunlight. Luke stared. In the dark shadows sat a lump with a blanket covering it. Must be more boxes. He'd never noticed them before stuck away and hidden.

Luke walked over and knelt on the floor, flinging away the dusty blanket. He sneezed as a daddy long-legs scuttled up the back wall.

The top box was heavy and slid awkwardly on its side with a thump. Luke opened the flaps. No wonder it was weighty. Books filled every inch of the box. He pulled out the first book. *Soccer Techniques and Strategies*.

Luke sucked in his breath, feeling dizzy. He reached for the second hardbound book, then a third. All the books were about soccer. Some were even coaching manuals. Luke laid them on the mattress, smoothing his hands over the slick pages.

Mama hiding soccer books in the storage shed? How could that be? First he found old soccer balls in Mr. Perea's shed. That made sense for an 80-year-old ex-soccer player. But now piles of soccer books in his very own shed? It was impossible. It was incredible. But the books were real. Very real.

Luke figured the answers had to be somewhere. He returned to the second box and began to dig. The glitter he'd seen earlier was a metal picture frame sticking halfway out of the top. He pulled it out and discovered that it was a studio portrait of his parents. Mama looked young and beautiful, dark hair flowing over her shoulders. Close to her, his father smiled easily. He was handsome, with thick dark hair and a full mustache. His brown eyes seemed to hold Luke's as though he could actually see him through the picture. It was weird. Tiny prickles ran up and down his arms. A confident, foreign glint glimmered in those eyes. This man wasn't like the fathers Luke saw at the school open house. Not a dad. It was more like his mother had posed for a picture with a stranger or a movie star.

At the very bottom of the box was a blue photograph album. Luke set it on his lap and opened the cover, expecting the pages to be full of his father and mother. But the first few pages held snapshots of himself as a baby. Pictures of Mama carrying him home from the hospital wrapped in a blue blanket decorated with elephants and ducks. He saw himself crawling, learning to walk, eating birthday cake with chocolate frosting stuck in his hair. Luke had never seen these pictures. Mama must have put them away years ago when he was young. She only kept his school pictures up on the walls now. The baby was like a stranger, too.

The baby pictures ended when he was about two. There were a few blank pages and then came the pictures Luke was searching for.

One photo showed his father leaning against a car wearing jeans and drinking beer. In another, his parents stood in front of an apartment building, their arms wrapped around each other.

Then, suddenly, the pictures made a switch. His father was gone. Luke frowned. Instead there were pictures of *soccer games*. Goalies hunched over in their goal boxes. The ball flying across the field, players poised in various running positions, legs kicking straight out. One player sprang upward to snag the ball.

Luke felt his arms go weak.

There were four full pages of soccer pictures. All taken from the stadium crowd, but on different days because the photographer had changed seats. A few were blurry and out of focus. Who took these pictures? His father?

Luke flipped the pages back and forth. There was something different between them. The uniforms had changed colors, but it was more than that. He couldn't pin it down. With a start, he realized what it was. The latter photographs had been taken in a foreign country.

In the first set, the stadium billboards advertised in English. In the second, all the billboards were written in Spanish. It made sense if his father lived in Mexico now. But these weren't recent pictures.

Luke stood up and slammed the photograph album shut. He went outside into the sunlight. His father must have really been nuts about soccer. Luke leaned against the scruffy elm tree next to the shed and kicked the bark with his heel. His father loved soccer, had gone to a lot of soccer games. Even bought a load of books. So what? But now Luke wanted to know why Ricardo Espinosa had left him and his mother. Why couldn't he have stuck around and taken his own son to a few soccer games? It wasn't fair that Paul Pickerell got to play *and* got to have his father coach the Fighting Falcons. Why couldn't he have the same thing Paul had?

Luke shoved his hands in his pockets. It was stupid to be mad. He shouldn't let a few dumb pictures ruin the pleasure of the soccer books.

He locked up the shed again and took the books into his bedroom, poring over the wonderful pictures and soaking them into his brain. An hour later, feeling itchy and restless, Luke got up and kicked the blue leather ball in a circle around the room, enjoying all the new space. Back and forth he sliced it between his feet. Then Luke leapt ahead to catch the ball before it hit the wall. He stopped it with his heel and shot it back against the opposite wall. By late afternoon he was sweating and went into the kitchen for a glass of water. Standing at the sink, the most incredible idea hit him.

Luke set the glass down and shook his head.

Whispers from the past buzzed in his mind.

A moment later he raced back to the shed and threw off the blankets. Furiously, he flipped the pages of the photograph album, back to the soccer pictures.

He stared at the players. Man by man. The faces blurred. Hurriedly, he went backward, excitement making him sweat. His stomach felt tight as a knot in a rope. The snapshots of his parents held a clue. He hadn't paid much attention earlier, but now he studied their clothing. His father was wearing jeans, but it wasn't a T-shirt under his jacket. It was a yellow jersey, a soccer jersey. Luke couldn't make out the number. The angle of his father leaning into his mother concealed the figures. Except for the edges. One number had a rounded border and looked like it might be a three or an eight.

Luke jerked the album pages back to the soccer games. He searched the numbers on the player's jerseys, but it was hard to see in the dim shed.

Impatient, Luke ran outside. There were no eights on any of the jerseys, but there *was* a three. Number forty-three on a yellow jersey. And the man on the field, running after the speeding soccer ball, had a faint, dark line above his mouth. It had to be a mustache.

That man was his father.

He was a professional soccer player.

And he played on a team in Mexico.

Luke peeled back the clear plastic and removed the snapshot, sticking it into his back pocket. An extraordinary feeling surged through his body. There was a reason he had such a drive. Such a longing to play soccer. He couldn't help it.

It was in his blood.

⚽ EIGHT

Luke locked the shed for the last time and put the key back in the drawer. He felt ready to explode. His mind raced with questions.

Plopping onto the couch, he tossed the blue-and-white soccer ball back and forth between his palms. Did his family live in Mexico when he was a baby? Why did his mother come back to the United States? His father must have stayed to play soccer. Why didn't he ever write or visit? He wasn't a drunk bum lying in a street. His father was a famous soccer player, and he must be rich!

Luke twirled the ball on his fingers. His mind spun with possibilities. Oh, what his father could teach him about soccer! That thought sunk deep. Luke paused and tucked the ball under his arm. From his back pocket he pulled out the picture he had taken from the album. Maybe it wasn't too late. Maybe he could still have what Paul had.

How much would it cost to go to Mexico City?

He could take a bus. That wouldn't cost too much, would it? Not like an airline ticket.

Luke bounced off the couch and dug the telephone book out of the kitchen drawer. He looked up the number for the Greyhound bus line and picked up the phone.

There were three rings before a voice drawled, "Greyhound, can I help you?"

Luke's stomach felt like he had a can of fishing worms wriggling inside, but he managed to keep his voice steady. "How much does it cost to take a bus to Mexico City?"

"You can't get there from here," the Greyhound man replied.

Luke's stomach dropped.

"First you take a bus to Juarez. Then you get a train into Mexico City."

"Oh. How much for a one-way ticket to Juarez?"

"Fifty bucks."

Luke gulped. "How much for a train ticket to Mexico City, do you know?"

The man gave a snort of laughter. "You'll have to call the train, kid."

Luke sagged against the counter. Fifty dollars. It might as well be five hundred dollars. And the train on top of that. What else did he expect? Mexico City must be more than a thousand miles away.

But it wasn't impossible. He wriggled the folded piece of paper out of his pocket. Calle de Piedra, Mexico.

He could write a letter to his father.

His father probably didn't realize how grown-up Luke was now. Or that he was dying to play soccer. If his father knew, wouldn't he jump at the chance to bring his son to Mexico?

He grabbed his school notebook and tore out a piece of lined paper. A new plan instantly formed in his mind. He could be on his way to Mexico City in a few weeks. His father would personally take charge of his future as a soccer player. Luke planned to work hard and be good. He had his father's genes, didn't he?

He rehearsed the trip in his mind. A bus from Albuquerque to Juarez. Passports, tickets. Did you take a lunch with you on a bus or did they stop at restaurants along the way? Then crossing the border, getting to the train station. A long overnight train trip into Mexico City would take hours. And everybody would speak Spanish. He didn't know much Spanish. But surely his father knew English. After all, he had lived in the United States once.

Luke found a stubby pencil and sat cross-legged in his hammock. He swayed back and forth for a minute, staring out the window and trying to think.

He plunged in.

Dear. And got stuck.

Dear who? Dear Father? Dad? Mr. Espinosa? This was tougher than he thought.

He finally settled on Dear Ricardo Espinosa. And the date at the top of the page like he had been taught in school.

Dear Ricardo Espinosa,

You probably do not remember me much since I was a little kid when I did know you, but I just turned twelve last month and I am in the Sixth grade. Mama and me are living in New

*Mexico. You probably know that already. I saw
your picture and I found your soccer books. I
love soccer, just like you. I thought maybe I could
come and visit you. Maybe even live with you.
My dream is to play soccer with you and learn
how to be a professional soccer player. Would
you please write to me? I could come anytime. I
could bring my school books, too. Please write
soon. I want to start learning soccer as soon as
possible.*

Love, your son, Luke

It took a long time to get the words right, but finally
Luke thought it sounded pretty good. He wrote it twice
more until there wasn't a single mistake, and his handwriting was neat the way Mrs. Schaffer liked. When
he got done his hand was tired. Writing letters was
hard work.

He folded the letter and put it in an envelope he found
in one of the kitchen drawers. Then he carefully wrote
Ricardo Espinosa and the address in Mexico City on the
front. In the upper left-hand corner he wrote his own
name and address and then stuck three stamps to the
right-hand corner to make sure he had enough postage.

There, it was done.

He slammed the front door of the trailer and ran all
the way to the village post office. When he slipped the
letter into the slot, Luke smiled. His stomach did a
series of flip-flops.

"Check *that* out, Pickerell," he said out loud. "And
watch where you drool."

⚽ NINE

On Sunday morning, Luke swung back and forth in his hammock thinking about the letter. He pictured it getting stuffed into a sack and taken in a truck to the airport, where it would get loaded onto a big jet and flown to Mexico City. He might be riding an airplane himself in just a couple of weeks!

Luke rolled out of the hammock and got dressed. Last night, he'd spent hours reading the stack of soccer books until he fell asleep. Now he had to try out some of the things he'd learned. But first, he had to hide the books from Mama. He couldn't tell her anything about it yet. Not until he got the letter back from his father asking for Luke to come to Mexico. Maybe Mama could come to Mexico, too! She could go to school there and open her beauty shop. Both their dreams could come true at the same time. It was so perfect. Luke could hardly wait for the letter to arrive.

He stashed the soccer books in a drawer of his dresser in the closet where he'd put it to make room for the hammock. They should be safe there.

In the kitchen, Luke ate some cold rice and a couple of tortillas, and that's when he realized his mistake.

He shouldn't have put his mattress and bed frame in the shed yesterday. When Mama came home late last night, she would have seen that it was gone. Would she guess why he wanted to put up the hammock? He had a strange, worried feeling as he kicked his ball around the floor of his room. When he heard Mama's bedroom door finally open, he stuck the ball under his pillow and went into the hall.

"There you are, Luke," she said.

He stood in front of her, feeling guilty.

Mama's dark hair was frizzy from sleep. She smoothed a hand down her pink robe. "You went into the shed yesterday."

"I just stuck my bed out there."

"Your hammock looks good," she admitted. "But it means you went into my room to find the key."

"I'm sorry, Mama."

She watched his face. "What else did you do in the shed?"

He swallowed. "Nothing. There's only some old clothes and tools."

Mama sighed. "You're right. There's nothing out there." She put a hand to her forehead. "Some of the waitresses are out with flu, and I have a headache, too. I'm going to lie down for awhile longer, then I have to go to the market. Stay out of trouble, and don't go into my room again."

"I won't," Luke promised.

She disappeared back into her room, and Luke let out his breath. He knew he'd have to tell her about the letter to his father. But he couldn't yet. Not until he had an airline ticket in his hands. He grabbed an apple and his soccer ball and pounded down the steps of the trailer. The morning was warming up, and until it snowed he wanted to practice outside.

He kicked the soccer ball toward the ditch banks, hoping to find a quiet place to practice. No cars or people.

"Luke!" someone called behind him. "Wait up, Luke!" He stopped the ball, stomach sinking.

Rosie rushed up breathlessly, pushing her baby in the stroller. "Hey, Luke, what you doing?"

It was too late to escape. Luke glanced down at the soccer ball under his foot and stared at Rosie's toes sticking out of a pair of sandals. Over her white blouse, she wore a green windbreaker that was too big. Probably her husband's. The baby had fallen asleep.

"Shouldn't you put him in his bed for a nap?" Luke asked.

"He loves to sleep in the stroller. It's the only way he stays asleep. Where you going?"

"Nowhere." He picked up the ball and put it under his arm.

"Ooh," Rosie said. "A soccer ball. Where'd you get it?"

"Nowhere," Luke repeated.

"Come on, Luke, tell me. Can I walk with you? I got nobody to talk to."

"Where's Ramón?"

"Out with his buddies. Sunday afternoon, and they were all drinking in the trailer so I told them to get lost. The baby was trying to sleep, but started crying cuz they got so loud."

Resigned to her company, Luke sighed, dropped his ball to the ground, and started to walk and kick again.

When they reached the ditch bank, Luke helped her lift the stroller up, and they kept going. The baby didn't even stir when the wheels bumped over the rocks in the road.

"Know what?" Rosie said. "Your Mama and me are going to study for the GED together. She said she'd get the study booklets, and on her days off we'll get together and learn all the stuff. When she cut my hair yesterday, she said she needs the GED certificate to get into beauty school. I'm so excited, I can't stand it."

Luke felt like kicking the ball clear over the trees to the river. Why hadn't Mama told him Rosie was going to be coming over on her days off?

"Now I won't have to think up reasons to come over and visit. Your Mama's so nice. She's probably my best friend. We're going to get real smart together." Rosie sounded like a kid who'd just been handed a present.

"What are you going to do with your GED?"

"We-ll," Rosie drew out the word with a long breath. "I might go to beauty school, too. With your mama. If Ramón lets me. She said if we both graduated, I could work in the shop she's going to get."

Luke didn't know if he could stand seeing Rosie every day for the rest of his life.

"There's something else I need to tell you. Actually, I'm *informing* everybody I know," Rosie said. "I'm going to be eighteen next month, and I decided I want people to call me Rosa. That's my real name. I've been called Rosie since I was a baby, and I'm not a kid anymore. I'm a married lady with a kid."

Luke kicked the ball, raising a cloud of dust.

"When Ramón and me got married last year, we had napkins with *Rosa and Ramón* printed in gold. Did I ever show you those napkins from my wedding, Luke? I got the idea from a lady on a talk show, and they looked all elegant and rich. Well, this morning I woke up and said, my name is Rosa Montoya from now on."

"What was it before?" Luke said.

Rosie rolled her eyes. "You *know* what I'm talking about. Can't a person change her name if she wants to?"

"Doesn't sound like you're changing it."

Rosie snorted and stuck her hands on her hips, eyeing him. "Hey, Luke. You looking for a good place to practice? I know a big old clearing up this trail. I'll show you." The stroller rattled over the dirt path as Rosie pushed onward, her thin, sticklike legs walking faster.

Luke hung back, tempted to lose her, but decided to see if maybe Rosie knew what she was talking about. They walked along for another quarter mile, twisting through the cottonwoods.

"See this little bend?" Rosie motioned. "It looks like a dead end, but if you go past this bunch of skinny elms . . ."

Luke followed the back of her green jacket into a little clearing. Blue sky peeked above the tops of the giant trees. Lemon-colored sunshine slanted through the branches. It was great. He dropped the ball to the ground and toed it around. Then he noticed Rosie watching him. Halting, he stuck his hands in his pockets and stared back at her.

"Can I stay and watch?" Rosie began to beg.

"I can't practice with you watching my every move."

"I'll stay out of the way. I'll go over here, see?"

"No," Luke told her.

"But I don't want to go home."

Luke folded his arms. He wasn't giving in. But he was saved from Rosie's stubbornness because just then the baby woke up and began to scream.

"Oh, fine," Rosie snapped. "See if I care." She heaved the stroller over a rock and stomped off.

Luke checked to make sure she was gone, then eagerly picked up the ball and positioned it between his hands. He let it drop and popped it with his foot. The ball bounced out of sight. That was stupid. Now he had to find it. He spotted the blue hexagons in the middle of a hedge.

Back in the clearing, he stripped down to his T-shirt, hanging the sweatshirt over a branch. When he kicked the ball again, he was careful not to boot too hard.

There was a rustling in the bushes. Luke froze and whipped around. "Come on, Rosie," he groaned.

But it wasn't Rosie. The ragweed swayed and a wet, pointed nose pushed through. Old Rex trotted over to Luke, the brown folds of his skin rippling over his bones.

Luke laughed and knelt to rub the dog's ears and face between his hands. "You silly old thing," he told the animal. "You never give up following me, do you?"

Rex panted, his tongue hanging out his mouth, but his tail kept thumping.

"It's a long walk, too," Luke said. "Hope I don't have to carry you back home."

After the old hound dog had his fill of Luke's vigorous petting, he lumbered across the clearing and lay down to watch.

Now Luke had an audience, even if it was only a dog. He didn't mind Old Rex, but it felt strange to have the dog watching him. Which the animal did, intently, following his every move as Luke kicked the soccer ball around the clearing. Rex never fell asleep. It was sort of like having a guardian.

At first, he felt awkward and the ball kept running off on him in all directions. He spent more time chasing it around the clearing than kicking it between his feet like he'd seen the soccer players do on television.

He kept at it, kicking in smaller movements to keep the ball under his control. After an hour, he could kick and run with the ball, keeping it just a couple of feet in front of him. He circled the entire clearing twice without losing the ball in the bushes. That's how he'd seen Paul dribble down the sidelines. It felt terrific.

After a few more times around the clearing, Luke decided to try something he'd read about in the soccer books. He made an imaginary circle around his body about five feet in diameter and pretended he was guarding the ball from the enemy team. An invisible player darted everywhere, trying to steal.

Luke moved the ball closer to his own goal. He shifted his position, keeping the ball away from the shadow of the enemy lurking over his shoulder. At the end of the clearing a monstrous, twisted cottonwood rose. Luke raced toward it. The other team was close on his tail, breathing down his neck. It was now or never. He gave the ball a swift, thudding kick and sent it slamming into the trunk. The ball bounced backward, flying into the air.

Luke was ready. He jumped up and caught it midair. "A point for the Pumas!" he yelled. That was Mr. Perea's favorite team in Mexico. His voice vibrated in the empty stillness and Old Rex barked, once, sharply. Luke glanced around, wondering if Rex's bark meant someone was in the area, but he was deep in the bosque and only a bird twittered. Probably nobody around for a mile.

Luke played another game, more aggressively this time, but he wasn't ready and the ball was harder to keep under control. Several times the ball hit rocks and bounced off into the bushes, but he didn't give up and dug into the shrubbery over and over again.

The sun rose higher in the sky, and Luke was starting to wear out. His heart hammered in his ears and his T-shirt was getting wet. One more kick and he'd take a break. Luke sped the ball along the ground and scored another point on his goal tree. Old Rex lifted his head and barked again. Luke glanced at the dog as the ball rebounded too high and soared over his head. Right into another wall of bushes.

Panting, Luke sat under the tree to catch his breath before chasing the ball down again. He and Rex watched each other across the clearing, Rex with his head lowered back down on his paws. "You funny, smart dog. I think you're barking every time I score on the cottonwood tree."

Old Rex just yawned.

Suddenly, out of nowhere, like it had just grown a set of wings, Luke's soccer ball came flying back through the air straight for him. He jumped up and got hit in the stomach.

"Ooooff!" Luke gasped, positive he was going to lose his breakfast.

The new girl from school stepped out from behind the bushes and grinned at him. She burst into giggles. "You should see your face! That soccer ball coming at you—had you going, didn't it?" In a spooky voice, she added, "The mysterious flying soccer ball."

"I—I thought you were Rosie," Luke said defensively.

"Who's Rosie?"

"She's just—a girl."

"Your girlfriend?"

"No!" Luke nearly shouted. "She's *not* my girlfriend. She's married. And she's got a baby. So what?"

"So, nothing."

They stared at each other for a moment. It felt strange to be together without the rest of the classroom around.

"So," Luke said, feeling a little ridiculous. "You're Amelia, right?"

"And you're Luke, huh?"

"You don't look like an Amelia."

She stuck her hands on her hips and leaned toward him. "What is an Amelia supposed to look like?"

"I don't know." He shrugged.

"You don't look like a Luke," she said in the same tone he had used. "Yeah, you look more like a George or something. Maybe Harry or Wallace. No, not Wallace. I once knew a Wallace and you don't look anything like him. He was extremely fat and always ate chocolate doughnuts."

Luke groaned, holding his stomach. "Chocolate doughnuts don't sound too good right now."

Amelia's face fell. "Hey, you okay? Sorry I got you with the ball. I was just playing a joke. Oh, what a great dog!"

Old Rex stood at attention under his tree. Luke followed Amelia over and she bent to pet him.

"He's getting pretty old, isn't he? Have you had him since you were little?"

"He's not mine," Luke told her. "His name's Rex and he belongs to my neighbor, Mr. Perea. But he's a pretty terrific dog. He follows me around whenever I go to watch the soccer games."

"Oh, yeah, I remember seeing him the other day at the fields. Followed you up the ditch, right?"

Luke nodded, a little uncomfortable. Had she really paid that much attention?

"You want to play some more soccer?" She brushed dirt from her stiff jeans.

"Well, it is hard to practice by yourself," Luke said. He didn't want to admit he hadn't played much before.

"It seemed like you were doing all right." She ran across the clearing and retrieved the ball, then expertly kicked it over to him.

Luke ran for it, but hit it wrong and the ball bounced crookedly off into the trees. He felt his face burn as he ran to get it.

But Amelia didn't seem fazed. A wrinkle of concentration creased her brow as she took the ball and positioned it on the ground. "I've always wanted to do some coaching," she said in a professional tone. "If you're running forward to catch a ball you want to hit it with the top of your foot. Right here." She pointed to the laces on her sneaker. "Just drive it straight down the field."

"I figured that much out."

"Okay. Say you're running across the field to intercept. That means you have to kick the ball with the side of your foot and still aim it toward your goal."

Luke nodded. "Right."

"You kick with the inside of your foot," she said, demonstrating with the ball on the ground. "If you catch it with your heel the ball will curve off wrong. Sometimes you want a curve, but it's awfully tricky. I still have to practice that move to get the ball where I want it to go. Ready to play?"

"I was using that tree for the goal."

"I'll kick it across the clearing. You run up and see if you can hit the tree, using a sidekick."

They got in position, and Amelia shot the ball across the dirt. Luke ran forward, trying to time his feet to arrive at the same moment as the ball. As the ball skimmed the ground, he ended up dancing in place, trying to decide which foot to use. His body wasn't straight either, and at the last second, he turned his right leg, trying to aim for the tree. The ball nicked the edge of his sneaker and bounced off. He wished Amelia hadn't shown up. She was a pro compared to him.

But all she said was, "Okay, try it again."

The second time was a little better, then Luke kicked a couple of rounds to Amelia. They took turns guarding the tree and running the ball in for a goal. Luke tried ten straight shots, deciding to save the side kicks until he could hit the tree head-on more consistently.

"Hey, that's great!" Amelia hollered after he smacked the cottonwood for the fifth time. Rex barked from his spot across the clearing.

A warm feeling swept from Luke's toes to his head. The last one *felt* great, solid. "It must be this new ball I just got."

Amelia laughed. "You either got ripped off or you found it in the garbage."

Luke smoothed back his dark hair and looked away. "Maybe I did."

"Everybody's got to start sometime," Amelia said, like it was no big deal.

"I've been setting up my room for practice. You know, for when it snows."

"Your bedroom?" Amelia asked. "How do you do that? I can't even walk into my room without falling over junk and clothes."

Luke palmed the ball between his hands. "I think it's going to work pretty good."

"My mom would never let me practice soccer in my bedroom. Of course, I'd have to kick my little sister out first."

"Where did you move here from?"

"Montana."

Montana seemed like a million miles away.

"I got to ride an airplane by myself. My parents drove the U-Haul." Amelia made a funny face. "I had to stay with my grandmother and start school. We haven't been to New Mexico in years. Since I was little. I don't remember my grandmother being so *old*. Luanne—that's my best friend in Montana—*her* grandmother is only forty-nine. She sunbathes in a bikini during the summertime and windsurfs on the lake. Mine can hardly walk. Actually, I threw a fit before we moved. My mom practically had to drag me onto the plane."

"Why?" Luke said, trying to keep up with her story.

"Because I had to miss two of my soccer games!" she hollered, as if the reason were completely obvious. "My parents think I'm obsessed. They make me use my allowance to pay for the registration."

Luke couldn't sympathize too much. An allowance. He wondered what that would be like.

"There's no city league teams here for girls my age. I guess this town's too small. They say there's a high school team, but that's almost four years away. I don't know what I'm going to do. Hey, do you live very close?"

Luke pointed to the south. "Over there in a trailer park."

"You mean Rio Grande Trailer Park?"

Luke nodded.

"Unbelievable!" Amelia exclaimed. "We're renting a trailer there, too, until my mother can find a house she likes. That means we're neighbors!"

A moment later Amelia was pulling him back home along the ditch banks, with Old Rex trotting behind. "Hey, why haven't I seen you walking to school?"

"I take the shortcuts along the ditches," Luke told her. "I don't go by the streets."

"Will you show me sometime?" Amelia asked.

"How'd you find the clearing in the bosque?"

"Just started exploring. If I have to live here, I figure I better find my way around. Show me where you live."

Luke dragged his feet, braking in front of the chain-link fence and thinking about their ugly trailer with its beat-up refrigerator and used furniture.

Still panting, Rex continued down the road and slunk under his porch to sit in the shade. "Good boy," Luke called to him, then turned to Amelia. "I don't think today's such a good idea—I, uh, it's not cleaned up."

"You should see my room," she said. "There's probably stuff growing under my bed."

"But, it's not—" he stopped, feeling a little helpless. No one had ever seen inside their place. Only Rosie, and her trailer was worse.

Amelia slowed down, matching his steps. She smiled at him. "I don't care. Hey, we're renting one of these yucky trailers, too."

Luke shot her a glance. Amelia seemed pretty nice. And she knew her soccer, that was for sure.

"Actually," Amelia went on as if nothing had happened, "I have my grandma to thank for getting me started with soccer. She gave me a ball for my fifth birthday. It came in a box, special delivery. I've been hooked ever since."

"See, she's not so bad," Luke told her.

Suddenly, Amelia whirled to face him. "I've got an idea! Let's go over to the soccer fields and watch the tournament tryouts."

Luke halted in the road. "I don't think so."

"Oh, come on," Amelia urged. "It's probably almost over anyway. There's nothing else going on in this little town."

Amelia dragged him along and Luke hoped Paul wouldn't see him. When they got there the field was covered with boys plus swarms of parents and coaches. The players had been divided by age, and the coaches on the committee were running them through rounds of various techniques. Dribbling, kicking, passing, goal defense.

"I wish I was out there," Amelia sighed. "Oh! There's Tomás from school. He's a classy player. I wish he wasn't so quiet. He doesn't even laugh at my jokes."

Luke smiled, feeling glad to be with this new girl from Montana.

"Hey, Tomás!" Amelia shouted, waving.

Now Luke was embarrassed. Tomás glanced over and nodded when he saw Amelia and Luke, then turned back to the coach, who was giving instructions on the next round of exercises.

Luke didn't see Paul until a soccer ball came whizzing through the air over their heads. Luke chased the ball to the fence and picked it up. When he turned to see which group had lost its ball, Paul crossed the sideline.

TEN

"**H**ey, Espinoso, give me back my ball."

Luke palmed the soccer ball for a moment, feeling the new, stiff leather, then tossed it over to the boy.

Paul caught it in the air with one hand. "Now you two sit back and watch the Falcon star."

"Your head's so big, I'm surprised you can stand up without falling over," Amelia told him.

"Watch your mouth, runt," Paul retorted.

"I may be short, but I bet I can outrun you," Amelia shot back.

Paul just laughed and returned to his group.

Sitting on the grass next to Amelia, Luke tried not to be envious of all the soccer going on around him. Every few moments, Paul glanced over at them, a grin on his face.

Coach Pickerell shouted, "Paul, quit daydreaming and pay attention!"

Luke watched Paul's face turn stony, and the boy bent over.

Amelia picked at the grass. "I hear Coach Pickerell's

getting Paul ready for the American Soccer League. Just like his brother, Phil."

"At least Paul's got help."

"What if Paul decides he doesn't want to?" Amelia said. "I heard Mike say they want to play football when we get to middle school next year, but his dad told him it would ruin his soccer career. You know, injuries, and not enough time to practice soccer."

Luke whistled softly.

Amelia leaned closer. "I heard him and Tomás talking during lunch last week. Coach Pickerell was going to stop paying for Phil's college tuition if he didn't get called for a national team."

Luke watched Paul out on the field. The boy's face was grim as he concentrated on the drills. Sometimes he didn't look very happy playing soccer.

"Coach Pickerell is one tough coach," Amelia said. "Sounds like he's an even tougher father."

Luke stood up to lean against the fence. He didn't care about Paul. How was *he* going to get out there on that field next season? The older teams wouldn't take a beginner, and he couldn't be on a team with six-year-olds.

Luke thought about the letter winging its way down to Mexico City, and he couldn't help smiling. That letter was just the beginning of making his dream come true. It was going to happen. He could feel it. After he trained with his father he'd come back next season and blow away the whole Falcon team. If he didn't end up staying in Mexico permanently.

Amelia rose from the damp grass and Luke followed her down the sidelines. The groups rotated drills. Paul's group moved to where the orange cones were set up for dribbling relays.

"Let's watch this," Amelia said.

Coach Pickerell divided the boys into four smaller groups. "Dribble down with the right foot, circle the cone, then dribble back with the left," he instructed. "Second split is just the opposite. Left foot, then right."

Paul's group was closest to the sideline, and Luke stepped out of the Falcon captain's range of vision.

Holding a clipboard and a pen, Coach Pickerell surveyed the teams, then blew his whistle for the start. The first four boys took off, dribbling as fast as they could. The others in line shouted them on.

"It's not a race," Coach Pickerell roared. "I'm watching your dribbling skills."

The boys slowed down for a second, but then sped up again, anxious to finish first anyway.

Paul danced in place, eager to run. He slapped his thighs and straightened his shin guards, then glanced at Luke.

By the time the third group began dribbling, the first team had fallen behind. The middle boy and Paul were neck and neck. Paul pulled ahead by a step.

Paul lunged ahead another half step as he rounded the orange cone, but he swung wide and was running on the edge of the white boundary.

"Come on, Pickerell!" his team screamed.

Luke felt like he was running the race right along with them. He inched closer to the sideline, his heart drumming, his legs straining to break free and run.

Suddenly, Paul's ball swerved over the line. Right in front of Luke.

Without thinking, Luke tapped the ball back over the line. Immediately, he could have kicked himself. He shouldn't have done it. And he had kicked too hard. The ball rolled past Paul and bounced into the second boys' running lane.

"Hey!" Paul screamed at Luke. Frantically, he ran after his ball. But the runner next to him had caught up and as Paul turned, the two boys collided and fell sprawling to the ground.

Yells of triumph pierced the air as the first boy flew past them both and won the relay.

"Uh, oh," Amelia said in a low voice.

Luke felt his stomach drop clear to his knees. Why did he kick that ball? Tapping the soccer ball had been like a reflex. He had just done it.

Paul picked himself up and brushed off his jersey. He came toward Luke, pointing his finger. "You did that on purpose."

"I'm sorry," Luke said. "I was just trying to help you keep the ball in bounds."

"I don't need your help," Paul hissed, stabbing his finger into Luke's shoulder. "Keep out of my way."

Coach Pickerell blew his whistle. "Get back here if you want to stay in the tryouts," he ordered his son. "It's your own fault. The ball was going out of bounds anyway."

The muscles in Paul's face twitched. "Yes, sir," he muttered. He glared at Luke one more time, then went back to his group.

"That's it, boys," Coach Pickerell said. "You've done all five rounds and tryouts are officially over. The tournament team members will be announced in about thirty minutes, so stick around." He walked to the side of the field where the other coaches were conferring over the final results.

Across the field, a hundred boys relaxed, some plopping onto the ground, exhausted, others goofing around with their balls.

"I wonder who will make the twelve-year-old team?" Amelia said.

"That's not hard to figure out," Luke replied. "Paul, Tomás, Mike, those three for sure. They always do."

A little later, the coaches formed a half-circle in the center of the field and instructed all the boys to sit in front of them.

One of the coaches blew his whistle. "Tournament practices begin the week after Thanksgiving and games start in January. There will be a total of eight tournament games and most will be played in Albuquerque. Two games will be overnighters in Gallup and Las Cruces. We'll begin with the seven/eight-year-old team." He proceeded to read off his clipboard. When he was finished, another coach stepped forward and called off the nine/ten-year-old tournament team.

Then Coach Pickerell raised his hand for quiet. "We have more boys playing this year than ever before in this age division, so those of you who have made the team before might not this year. Okay, here we go. Tomás Abeyta, Mike Burrell, Tony Draper, José Gurulé, Alfredo Mondragón, Phillip Otero, Kenny Reaves, Nacho Sanchez, Joseph Spaulding, Ralph Valerio, and Brad Wells."

The air was filled with cheers and a few boys stood up and whistled.

Amelia stared at Luke. "Paul didn't make the team."

"But his best friend Mike did," Luke said. "Let's get out of here." They started to cross the field but Paul followed them and grabbed Luke's arm from behind, swinging him around.

The Falcon captain breathed heavily in Luke's face. "It's your fault, Espinoso. You made me lose the relay. I'm not on tournament because of you."

Amelia had no sympathy. "Don't be a poor sport."

Luke winced, wishing Amelia would keep her mouth closed.

"You heard your dad," she added. "He said there was a lot of boys. Maybe he's giving somebody else a chance to play tournament this year."

"But I'm the best," Paul insisted, gripping Luke's shoulder. "It was because of *you.*"

Luke tried to shrug the boy's hand off.

Paul's pale blue eyes drilled into Luke's face. "I know why you kicked that ball. You're always trying to show me up in front of everybody. The art picture, and now the tournament."

"I'm sorry you didn't make the team," Luke said.

"You don't know nothing about nothing!" Paul spit out. "You're lucky I don't smash your face in, Espinoso." He held up a clenched fist and shoved it close to Luke's nose. "You want to go home bleeding?"

Luke's heart thudded in his throat. "I don't want to fight you, Pickerell. I didn't mean to mess you up by kicking the ball."

"I'll spare your face this time, but we're not finished. You think you're a hotshot to interfere with my soccer playing, so this is the deal. You and me will play a little one-on-one. Next Saturday."

Luke felt like Paul had just knocked him over. Play Paul? One-on-one? He wanted to sink into the earth.

Beside him, Amelia sucked in her breath. Luke could feel her eyes on him, waiting to see what he would say.

How could he admit that he didn't know how to play? There was no way he could play Paul, not yet, and if he tried he'd look like a fool. The Falcons, the other boys, Marcie and all the girls, would laugh at him. He might as well drop out of school and wash dishes for Mr. Perea.

"Sure, I'll play you," Luke said softly, trying to hide the jiggle in his voice. He didn't even know where the words were coming from. "But not one-on-one. A real game. My team against yours." Now he knew he was crazy. Whatever possessed him to say that?

Paul let out a laugh. "Your team, huh? What team? You on some *secret* soccer league? I'd like to see that." All of a sudden Paul was in a better mood. "You know, we can still get in that 'one-on-one' sometime during the game."

"I'm sure we will," Luke said, his heart sinking.

Paul's eyes gleamed. "Espino*so*, you are a bo*zo*."

⚽ ELEVEN

Amelia stared at Luke. "I can't believe you just did that."

Luke felt sick to his stomach. "Me, either."

"What are you going to do?"

"I don't know, but I have to go home," Luke said. It was late and he hadn't checked on Mr. Perea yet. Plus, he didn't feel like talking right now. "See you at school."

"If not before," Amelia said, and smiled as if she had some secret plan of her own. Amelia turned again and yelled. "Hey, Luke, I live in number nineteen on Torres road. That way!" She punched the air with her finger, pointing to the end of the street. He nodded and swung up the porch steps.

Amelia's voice rang through the air again. "Hey, Luke! You got it?"

He laughed and raised a hand in the air. "Okay, I got it!"

But once inside the trailer, Luke hit the couch with his fist, sending up a spray of old dust. The trailer felt too small for all the fears that swirled inside his head.

He had a week to learn soccer as well as Paul. A week to get up a team that could play Paul's team. It was impossible. It was a joke.

He paced the floor the rest of the day, popping his ball, stomach in knots, and trying to be quiet while Mama was sick in her room. He couldn't even enjoy reading the soccer books when he got into bed that night. It was too hard to concentrate. He had crazy dreams all night long of playing Paul. The Falcon captain kept smashing his face into the soccer field until Luke disappeared right into the earth.

The next morning Mama was running around, grabbing her coat and purse. "Harry called and said three girls are out with the flu. He'll pay me time and a half if I do a twelve-hour shift."

"But you spent yesterday in bed yourself," Luke told her.

"I think I'm better. All that sleep must have done some good," she said, but she still looked tired. "I can't say no to time and a half. Not when I'm going to pick up the study booklets for the GED today." She twisted her hair into a bun with one hand. "I can't believe I'm really going to do it, Luke. Now get dressed or you'll be late for school." She kissed his cheek and was gone.

Still wearing his pajamas, Luke sat at the kitchen table with his cereal bowl and tried to picture his father's house. Big and fancy like a mansion, probably. Red tile hallways and a fountain in the front yard. He imagined his father arriving home from soccer practice in sweats and a bandanna, thumbing through the pile of mail.

He would find Luke's letter, and smile through his

mustache as he read it. The letter would make him realize how much he missed his son and how proud he was to know Luke wanted to follow in his footsteps as a soccer player. Right away, Ricardo Espinosa would sit down to write a letter back, before he even took a shower. Or maybe he would just pick up the telephone. What would it be like to hear his father's voice on the end of the line? Was it possible to get on a plane before Saturday and never have to play Paul?

Luke had thought about going to Mexico so much the night before it seemed to have worn a groove on his brain. Maybe he should call the airport and get a reservation just in case. He'd be ready as soon as his father sent for him. But he still had to tell Mama. He dreaded doing that. She didn't know that Luke had written the letter or found the photo albums. She might not let him go. No. He pushed the thought away.

Luke imagined himself in the stadium in Mexico City, playing with his father's team. The turf was cushiony and green. Huge lights shone as bright as daylight under stars that glittered in a black sky.

Closing his eyes, Luke brushed a hand against the uniform that his father would be sure to give him the moment he arrived. A blue jersey and white shorts, same colors as his ball, but crisp and new. He also had stiff, brand-name sneakers to help him run without slipping.

Luke could even see his father's teammates. Tall and handsome and muscular. Their black hair flew, wet with sweat, as they ran and dribbled and passed and kicked. Spanish floated on the air.

Ricardo Espinosa passed the ball to Luke. They were

both playing forward and worked the ball together back and forth across the field toward the goal. They smiled at one another, synchronized in their playing, like a perfect match. Now Luke dribbled through the maze of other players, right down the center. The opposing team raced beside him, trying to steal.

When Luke reached the entrance to the goal box, he kicked with all his might. His body wrenched forward. The ball sailed through the air. It was a perfect—

Bong! Bong! Bong!

Somebody was hitting the doorbell over and over again.

Luke looked down. His corn flakes were soggy.

The bell rang again.

He pushed back his chair. "Who's there?"

"It's Amelia. Who else? You still in bed?"

"No, wait a minute—"

"Open the door," she demanded. "Some old man's staring at me from his window next door."

"That's Mr. Perea. Wait." Luke ran down the hall and pulled on his jeans. Amelia was still ringing the bell. And knocking with her fist, too. It sounded as if there were ten people outside instead of just one. Amelia almost fell into the house when Luke finally opened the door, as if she must have been leaning against it. In one hand she held a plastic bag, and in the other her school pack.

"You were still in bed, huh?" she accused.

"I was eating breakfast."

Amelia examined the bowl of corn flakes. "Looks pretty yucky now."

"I forgot to finish," Luke said, thinking about the

point he'd almost made inside Aztec Stadium a few minutes ago.

"You also forgot to brush your teeth and comb your hair."

Luke put up a hand self-consciously. "You're not my mother. Or my sister."

"Your house is sure quieter than mine. My sister's always yelling about something. Where's your mom?"

"At work," Luke said. He thought a noisy house would be nice for a change.

"Where does she work?"

"Harry's Bar & Grill."

"We went there for dinner the first night my parents arrived. Can I see your hammock?" Eagerly she followed him down the hall. "Wow! This is terrific! How lucky. My mother would never let me set up my room like this."

Amelia didn't know what lucky was. She'd been playing soccer since she was five. He had a lot of years to make up. But now, with his father, everything was going to be different.

"Where's a ball?" Amelia begged. "I gotta try this out."

Luke handed over his old blue ball.

She palmed it, kicked it around the room, and bounced it against the wall. Then she jumped up to try out the hammock, and spilled the pile of soccer books he pulled out of his closet when Mama left for work. "Oops, sorry. Hey, where'd you get all these books about soccer? I've never seen these in the library, and believe me, I've looked."

Luke watched her thumb through the pages of photographs and illustrations. He sat down next to her and picked one up, too, getting a shivery tingle. His father had held these same books in his hands. "These books were my father's," he suddenly told her. "He's a soccer player."

Amelia looked up and her jaw dropped. "As in *professional* soccer player?"

Luke nodded.

"Well, where is he? Can I meet him?"

"He lives in Mexico and plays on one of the national teams."

Amelia whistled between her teeth. "Wow, how exciting! I want to get on the women's national team someday, or the pros, or maybe even the Olympics!" She picked up the ball again and dribbled it around the room in a circle. "This is great. Whoops!" The ball bounced off the wall and landed in the hammock. She scooped it out and kicked it back to Luke.

He stopped the ball with his foot and tried to bounce it into the air without his hands. He'd seen others do it, but he hadn't succeeded yet.

"I almost forgot!" Amelia cried. She ran over and opened the plastic grocery store bag. "It's a present. I brought you a pair of my old shin guards. I figured you didn't have any with that old ball of yours. So here, they're yours."

Luke hesitated. Mama had a lot of pride about taking handouts from others. Besides, things were different now.

"Go on," Amelia urged. "I cleaned them up and everything. I don't need them because I got a new pair this season."

"I don't think I'll need them, either," Luke said slowly. "I'm planning to go to Mexico. My father will be giving me everything I need to play. He's going to teach me and I'll be living down there."

"You are one lucky guy," Amelia said, jealousy creeping into her voice. "Well, you can use these in the meantime."

"No, thanks. I can get my own pair." He looked away.

Amelia dropped her hands and the bedroom went quiet. "Listen, Luke," she said evenly. "My mom would be really mad if she knew I was giving these away. My little sister's supposed to use them after me. I had to sneak them out of the house."

Luke lifted his shoulders. He'd love the shin guards, but it didn't matter anymore. And he couldn't get too friendly with Amelia. He was leaving for Mexico any day.

She sounded confused. "I was trying to help you out."

"You don't need to help me."

"Okay," Amelia's voice began to quiver. "Go down to Mexico and get your equipment from your pro father. See if I care. I was going to help you learn how to play against Paul. Not anymore, I guess."

Luke shook his head. "I'm not playing Paul. I'm getting out of here real soon. The sooner the better." The words sounded mean, but he couldn't seem to stop them from coming out of his mouth.

"What is your problem, Luke Espinosa?" Amelia demanded.

"When I get to Mexico I can learn real soccer from the pros."

"Real soccer? What's that supposed to mean? You trying to tell me what we're playing is *not* real?"

"You know what I mean," Luke said lamely.

"Right. I know what you mean. I get it." Shoving the shin guards back into the plastic bag, Amelia sniffed and turned away. Then she stomped down the hall and slammed the front door.

Luke stayed in the bedroom, fingering his ball. He hadn't meant to make her mad. The whole conversation had turned out wrong. But it didn't matter. Nothing mattered but Ricardo Espinosa and his team in Mexico City. He was going to be a pro soccer player. Just like his dad. By next week he'd have to forget about Amelia anyway. He'd be long gone. Away from Amelia, Rosie, Mr. Perea and all the cooking and cleaning, and mostly away from Paul Pickerell.

⚽ TWELVE

It was hard to concentrate on schoolwork. Luke's thoughts buzzed like a swarm of mosquitoes around a light. The letter. The fight with Amelia. Paul's challenge.

Luke picked up his pencil and began copying the week's spelling words on his paper. His fingers itched to throw down the pencil and caress his soccer ball. See if he could twirl it on his fingertips without dropping it. As he painstakingly wrote *international* in cursive, he shuffled an imaginary ball on the floor under his desk.

He looked up when Amelia rose from her seat and started to come his way. But as she brushed past his desk on the way to the pencil sharpener, she didn't even look at him. Not even a glance.

Luke gazed at the back of her yellow, wispy hair during free reading time, willing her to turn around and smile. She finally did turn once, but her eyes looked right through him. Like he didn't exist. He tried not to care. After all, hadn't he convinced himself he couldn't like her too much?

When the bell rang for recess, Paul stepped in front

of Luke and blocked the aisle. "You are one lucky dude, Espinoso," he said.

Luke backed up. "What do you mean?"

"There's good news and there's bad news. The good news is the Falcons are ready to eat you alive," Paul told him. "But my dad says we can't have the field or a referee until soccer season is over. We have to wait one more week. But maybe you're not so lucky. That's another whole week you gotta sweat it out until we smear your team all over the field."

"I'm not sweating," Luke said, hope surging. Another week gave him more time to get to Mexico. "Are you sweating, Pickerell?"

Paul just laughed. "Hey, where's your soccer drawing, Espinoso?"

"I turned it in to Mrs. Schaffer," Luke told him.

Paul's eyes narrowed. "But you were going to do a different drawing."

Luke shook his head. "I never said I'd do a new one."

"You like to make my life miserable, don't you, Espinoso? But soon *you're* going to be miserable." Paul grinned and walked out the classroom door.

Luke sank into his seat. Please hurry and write to me, he silently urged his father. If the letter came in a few more days he'd never have to play against the Falcon captain and humiliate himself in front of everybody. He'd be long gone, and boy, wouldn't they be jealous?

Luke spent his afternoons in the bosque with his soccer ball and Rex. He loved the feel of the leather against his toes and the cold wind in his mouth as he ran. He practiced and tried not to worry about Paul's challenge.

Even if he never played Paul he wanted to get better for his dad so he wouldn't look like such a beginner.

Every time he hit the cottonwood tree, scoring an imaginary goal, Rex barked from his spot under the trees. It was like praise or a thumbs-up from a best friend. And best of all, a letter had to be coming from his father soon. He started checking the post office box every day after school for a letter. He couldn't miss it. There wasn't a day to lose.

On Friday during lunch recess, Luke sat under a tree, wishing he had his soccer ball. A game of kickball was going on at the baseball field. A group of girls jumped rope. Amelia ran by, headed toward the field. Luke looked up, hoping for a sign of recognition. But Amelia didn't even share a split second of a glance.

Luke missed playing soccer with her. He even missed her Montana accent. She never showed up at the clearing again, but he hadn't expected her to after hurting her feelings. He tried not to think about her. He liked her too much.

After school, Luke grabbed the mail key from its kitchen nail and walked down Main to the post office. Should he have sent a picture of himself? Suddenly Luke couldn't remember what he had written. Had his letter sounded stupid and babyish?

He pushed open the glass doors, and there was Paul standing in front of the out-of-town slot, stuffing envelopes through the slit. Luke stopped short.

Paul gave Luke a slow, knowing smile. It drove Luke crazy, and Paul seemed to know it. He pointed to Luke and then himself and held up one finger. Soon, he was saying. Soon it would be just the two of them on the field. One-on-one.

Luke thought he'd rather die a slow death.

The Buick sedan parked at the curb honked its horn. Paul finished his errand and opened the outside door.

Coach Pickerell had opened the driver's door and stood in the road, his hands on top of the car. "Hurry up, what's taking so long?" he yelled. "You know the rule. Soccer players that dawdle have to practice an extra hour. And they don't stay champs very long," he added.

Paul's face was sullen as he glanced back at Luke, then slammed the post office door shut. Paul climbed into the Buick and Luke watched them drive away.

He shook his head to forget about Paul and took a deep breath. Was today the day for the letter? He was getting to be a regular customer in here, sometimes checking before school as well as after.

Luke stuck his mail key into the lock and opened the little door.

His breath whooshed out in a rush. There it was. A blue envelope. Long and narrow with a foreign stamp. Luke pulled it out from the pile of bills and just held it in his hands. His heart thudded so hard he could scarcely breathe. He didn't have to play Paul and die a slow death.

But he couldn't open it here. Luke slammed the little door shut, locked it, and raced back home, leaping over the ditch banks. He pounded up the trailer steps, slammed the front door, flung the rest of the mail on the kitchen table and dashed into his bedroom. Even though he was alone in the trailer he felt like having privacy. He jumped up into the hammock and sat in the middle. The sides folded in like a comforting hug.

Ricardo Espinosa's handwriting was bold and black.

His own name, Luke Espinosa, sprawled across the front of the envelope, looking big and important. Luke carefully tore the end and pulled out a sheet of thin, crinkly paper.

Dear Luke,

I was very surprised to get your letter. I haven't seen you since you were a baby. I'm sorry to know that you aren't getting along with your mother and you want to come live with me. I'm afraid that's impossible. She has custody of you and I'm not going to interfere with that.

Shortly after your mother and I separated ten years ago, I married my wife Maria. We have three boys, and they all play soccer, too. I think it must be in the genes. I coach the older boys' teams on my time off. José is nine, Manuel is seven, and Pedro is five. It wouldn't be right for you to come here. My life with your mother was over a long time ago.

I wish you all the best.

Ricardo Espinosa

P. S. It's nice to know you like soccer. I had my final season last year. I retired and am managing the team now. The Pumas hope to get in the finals for the World Cup. Watch us on the television!

⚽ THIRTEEN

The whole world seemed to stop. The birds outside the open window fell silent. The bedroom was deadly quiet. Even Luke's heart seemed to stop beating, hanging suspended in time. Finally he let out his breath, and the ragged hoarseness sounded foreign to his ears.

Luke crammed the letter into his pocket and grabbed his ball. He jumped down out of the hammock, slammed the front door, and raced for the bosque. His legs pumped up and down like pistons. His shoes thumped and slapped the hard ground.

When he reached the clearing, Luke hurled the ball with both hands against the monstrous gnarled cottonwood. He caught it and heaved it against the tree again. When the ball snapped backward, Luke lifted his foot and kicked it as hard as he could, crushing the old ball into the rough bark. It bounced crookedly and flew lamely into the bushes.

Bending over, Luke gasped, sucking in air like a drowning person sucks in water. His stomach hurt, his nose was running, and he couldn't seem to see straight.

Slowly, legs trembling, he went searching for the ball and found it under a tall hedge of messy elms. The poor soccer ball had taken such a pounding, it had lost air. Luke squeezed it, leaving thumbprints in the blue hexagons.

Shaking, he fell onto the dirt under the bushes, sticking the beat-up ball between his feet. The sun was warm, but the ground was cold. Dry leaves crackled under his jeans. The breeze grew stronger and cottonwood leaves floated silently down from the giant trees. The pale sunlight made the leaves look gold. Gold and blurry.

With the edge of his T-shirt, Luke wiped the water out of his eyes. He wasn't going to cry. He *wasn't*. But he sat there and didn't move. Just stared at the pathetic, old soccer ball and thought maybe he'd sit there forever. That's all he was good for. Maybe Mr. Perea was right. Dreams only existed to fall apart and dissolve. Some people were just not meant to have their dreams come true.

Luke pulled the letter out to read it once more. But the words hadn't changed. And now he had three half-brothers who were exactly like Paul. He hadn't known he could feel so sick. It was amazing how a piece of paper could be just like a knife twisting in your heart.

He should be on a plane to Mexico City by now. And here he was. Stuck. More than stuck. He had to play Paul, which meant he was going to be totally humiliated. Worse than dead. After Saturday, he'd never be able to show his face on a soccer field again.

Luke buried his head into his knees. He sat there for so long the sun began to drop and he got cold, but still he couldn't move. He thought he must have turned into a statue when an army of black ants began to march over his sneakers. A spider scuttled nearby and the wind moaned through the trees like someone crying.

When Luke finally looked up, late afternoon shadows were creeping down the empty ditch banks. Maybe he could live here in the bosque. Mama could visit him. Rex could keep him company. He could fish in the river for food.

As the sun disappeared behind the mesa, Luke shivered. What a stupid idea. It was just more dreams, more fantasy. He had been stupid to think his father would want him. Dumb to believe his dad would help him.

He felt like a stiff popsicle as he got to his feet, stuck the ball under his arm, and started the long walk home. When he got there the living room was empty, but he knew Mama was home because he spotted her purse on the counter. He went down the hall and found her sitting on the floor of his bedroom, rummaging through the closet.

Luke's heart pounded as he watched her toss the soccer books out one by one. *"Uno, dos, tres, quatro, cinco. Cinco! Cinco libros de soccer! Dios mío!"* Luke could see the splotches of ketchup and grease that decorated the front of her waitress uniform.

Luke licked his dry lips. "Mama, what are you doing?"

She jumped at the sound of his voice. "I came in to get your laundry, and I found these! You lied to me about the shed—" she paused and stood up, looking hard at him. "I am very upset."

"I'm sorry, Mama," Luke said slowly. "But why didn't you tell me he played soccer?"

She didn't answer for a moment. Her face changed from anger to weariness. "*No sé.* I don't know. I guess I have lied to you, too. I should have set fire to those books years ago, but I could never bring myself to destroy a book. I threw out the trophies he left behind, but that's all he left. Not much else. You were barely born when he got the offer to play for the Pumas in Mexico City. I gave up my home and my family to go with him, but soccer was his life. More than me. I never thought he'd make the professional team. I was sure he'd stop playing after the university, get a real job. I was young and stupid. And then your grandmother got sick. I've told you how we came back, just the two of us. I took care of her and she was sick for months and months—" Mama's voice broke. "I was so heartbroken and ashamed, I could never tell you the whole story."

Luke watched her, feeling rooted to the floor. Mama reached out a hand and touched his face, then dug her fists into the pockets of her uniform.

"Things changed. It shouldn't happen, but it does. Ricardo met Maria. I think she was the sister of another teammate and hung around the field watching the players. It's—crazy, but I loved him so much I couldn't hate him. Instead I hated the soccer. It took him away from me. How could you want to play soccer, Luke? Football, baseball—anything but soccer."

Luke swallowed past the thickness in his throat. "I

found his address in your book and I wrote a letter to him."

"*Qué?* What? Why did you do that? *¡Ay, Dios mío!*" Mama crossed herself on the chest, and her hands trembled. "I hoped this would never happen, but I should have known." She looked up, studying his room with new eyes. "The hammock—" she almost laughed. "I hear you bumping around the room before you go to bed. You are playing soccer in here, *qué no?*"

Luke dug out the slip of paper from his pocket and handed it to her.

"What's this, *hijito?*"

"He wrote me a letter back."

Slowly, she took the thin blue paper and unfolded it. "I recognize his handwriting," she whispered, skimming over the words.

Luke watched her eyes move back and forth across the sheet. It took so long he figured she read it about five times over. Just as he had the first time.

Finally, she folded the letter back up and put a hand on her chest. "I've been foolish for ten years. He has never helped, never written. Too guilty to ever come back and look me in the eye." She paced the floor, crumpling the letter in her fist. "And three babies! *Dios mio.* Luke, I'm sorry his letter is so cruel. I'm sorry for your dreams. We both have dreams, don't we? Dreams that will never happen."

Luke wanted to shut his ears. He didn't want to hear that. He didn't want it to be true.

She crossed the bedroom and fiddled with the top button of her work dress. Faint lines creased the corners of her eyes. "I'm going to change clothes and walk down to the laundry. Would you gather your dirty things?"

"Sure, Mama." He paused. He couldn't let it all go. He couldn't just forget about it. He had to tell her everything. Even his father's letter didn't shut off the burning dreams. "Mama?"

"*Sí?*"

Luke nearly stumbled over the words. "I love playing soccer. I have a friend who's teaching me. I wanted to go to Mexico. I wanted my father—him to teach me. I think I wanted the easy way, but I can't stop. I'm going to play, and I'm going to be good. I even found my own ball."

"*Verdad?* The same place you found the hammock? But aren't you too old to start playing, son? You told me all the boys have been playing for years."

"I'm going to learn anyway. Now I have to make the dream come true by myself."

Mama sighed, one hand on the doorknob. "But mine won't, baby. I think I have to face the reality."

Luke shook his head. She couldn't give up either. "It will, Mama."

"I haven't checked my bank account in a long time. It makes me too sad the way it grows so slowly. I still put a little in when I cash my check, but I haven't looked in months. I'm too tired to work all day and night and go to school also. If soccer is really what you want, let's take the money and buy a uniform and a new ball. What else do you need? Those leg things?"

"Mama, I don't need a uniform yet. I know where I can get some leg things," he added. "You call the beauty school Monday and register for classes."

"What? Oh, *mi hijo*, I can't. All those high-class ladies. Besides, they won't let me in. I still have to get my GED."

"I'll make you a bet," Luke said boldly.

"Hush, don't say that. God will hear you." She crossed herself and looked toward the ceiling, closing her eyes. But immediately she opened her eyes again. "What kind of bet?"

"I'll teach myself how to play soccer in the next week and you call the beauty school. We can do homework together."

"What's the bet?"

"Mint chocolate chip ice cream."

Cristina Espinosa laughed. "It's a deal, but I think it will take me a week to get my courage."

"It's going to take me longer to learn soccer," Luke said.

"But why do you need to really learn soccer in a week?"

"I have to. I have a game next Saturday."

⚽ FOURTEEN

After supper, Luke sat in his hammock, palming his ball. He'd wasted enough time waiting for someone else. Waiting for letters and dreams to come to him. For someone who wasn't even there. But he needed courage, just like Mama.

Last week, he had pretty much told Amelia to get lost. He knew he'd hurt her and if he tried to talk to her she might just slam the door in his face. But Luke needed her help. He couldn't play Paul without her. And he missed her.

Luke hoped he'd know the right things to say once he got to her house. But it was going to be hard. One of the hardest things he'd ever done. His life seemed to be full of hard, tangled things right now. But he'd only gotten himself into the messes.

He slid off the hammock and got his coat. Mama and Rosie were at the kitchen table, poring over the study booklets for the GED. Rosie's baby sat in the middle of the living room floor on a blanket, drooling over a graham cracker.

Mama frowned, flipping the pages. "This math looks

too hard. All kinds of words and numbers. Look at this one. Do you know how to do it?"

Rosie shook her head, watching Cristina Espinosa anxiously. "Beats me. I'll ask Ramón."

Luke's mother chewed her lip. "Maybe we need a tutor for the math part."

"I'll help you when I get back, okay?" Luke said. They went on to the English Grammar section as Luke closed the front door.

The evening was cold. Frost sparkled on the frozen ground. A lone streetlight cast a pale yellow pool in the darkness. Luke thrust his hands into the pockets of his jacket.

Number nineteen was a white trailer about halfway down the third dirt street. It was surrounded by a chain-link fence; a cracked concrete path led from the gate to the front door. Inside the fence was a dog. A little gray terrier lay under the rickety porch steps. The dog's chin rested on his paws and he raised his head as Luke headed to the gate. Yapping like crazy, ears straight up, the terrier quickly jumped to his feet and bounded across the yard. The dog reached the gate the same moment Luke did.

They stared at each other. The terrier continued barking, its tail wagging like a flag in a stiff breeze.

Luke bent over. "Good dog, good boy." He unlatched the gate cautiously, double-checking the number on the front of the trailer, and stepped inside the gate. He wiped his hands on the back of his jeans. Nerves made his palms sweat.

Panting with excitement, the animal leapt onto

Luke's leg. "Hey boy," Luke murmured, petting the dog's silky head.

He reached down to the prancing, nipping terrier. "Down boy!" Luke managed to get to the front door before the dog could jump onto his leg again.

After he knocked, a few moments passed without an answer. The dog stood at attention near Luke's heels, and it made him smile. The animal gave another series of sharp barks just as the door whipped open.

Behind the door, Amelia stood dressed in faded jeans and a T-shirt that had a picture of a crocodile on the front with its mouth gaping open. Rows of teeth glittered and the little beady eyes seemed to inspect Luke hungrily. Amelia was barefoot and eating a piece of bread. A blob of strawberry jam started to slip off the crust and Amelia stuck out her tongue and licked it up. She crammed the rest of the bread into her mouth and chewed, staring at Luke.

Luke's mouth had gone dry. Amelia didn't say anything and he couldn't seem to, either. The terrier barked and jumped up on Amelia's legs, trying to reach her face.

"Hello, Scotty," Amelia cooed. She bent over and cupped the dog's ears with her hands. "Are you hungry? Go get Jenny," she ordered, motioning him into the house.

The dog didn't need a second invitation. Panting eagerly, Scotty raced into the house.

"Who's Jenny?" Luke asked.

Amelia pursed her mouth and narrowed her eyes. She looked as if she was trying to decide whether to talk to him or not. "My little sister," she finally answered. "She's watching a Disney video and eating a dog biscuit."

"Dog biscuits?" Luke wasn't sure he heard her right.

Amelia leaned against the doorjamb and folded her arms. "Yeah, she loves them. But my mom limits her to one a day. She and Scotty eat them together. For a snack. Jenny's only four. Haven't you ever tried one? I thought every kid did when they're little."

"I never had a dog," Luke said.

Amelia raised an eyebrow and glared at Luke. Like she'd just remembered she wasn't on speaking terms with him. "Wanna make something of it?"

"No," Luke said quickly. "Jenny can eat them all day if she wants."

"What's *that* supposed to mean?"

"Nothing, I just mean—" Luke didn't know what he meant. He stopped and stared at the cracked concrete under his feet.

Amelia waited. "Well?" she finally said impatiently. "What do you want?"

It was clear Amelia was going to make him eat dirt.

"I'm sorry about—"

Amelia jumped in at the same moment. "I thought you'd be in Mexico City by now. Living high and mighty and learning *real* soccer from all those pros your dad knows."

"I'm not going."

"I thought it was all planned. Have to wait for your new luggage to arrive?"

Luke looked off to the side. "Can't you let a person say he's sorry without making it worse?" He stuck his hands in his jacket and slowly started down the steps.

A moment later he heard Amelia pound down the porch steps. "Hey, wait a minute, Luke."

He turned because he didn't really want to leave.

"What do you mean, you're not going? You mean never?"

Luke shook his head, not trusting his voice.

"I'm sorry," Amelia said softly.

He jerked his head to flick his dark hair out of his eyes and shrugged as if he didn't care.

They stood in silence again.

"So, why did you come over?" Amelia finally asked.

"I need you to teach me how to play soccer," Luke told her. "For real."

"You mean *real* soccer?" Her mouth twitched at the corners.

This was the Amelia he knew and liked. "The real thing. The whole thing."

She grinned. "So, like, you need my expert services? Paul Pickerell, huh?"

She was quick. Luke swallowed past the lump in his throat. "He says he's going to cream our team all over the field."

"Our team?" she squeaked. "Oh, man, you're in trouble."

"I'd like to leave town, actually," Luke said soberly.

That made her giggle. "Oh, you should see your face. You look so serious. But what are you going to do? You don't have a team."

He didn't hesitate for a second. "Amelia, you want to be captain?"

She grinned so wide her molars showed. "I'd love to get on the field with Paul Pickerell's team. But who else are we going to get? The other boys at school play on different teams for city leagues. They're not going to want to play with us."

Luke looked her in the eye. "I guess it'll be the boys against the girls."

Amelia threw her head back and gave a yell. "This game is going to go down in history!" She rapped her hand against her head, thinking hard. "Oh, this is going to be great! I hope it doesn't snow."

Snow was exactly what Luke was hoping for. Blizzards every day. Snowbound until spring.

"I need to get some soccer equipment," Luke said. "Want to go down to Goodwill with me tomorrow after school?"

Amelia opened her mouth in surprise, then shut it. "Uh, sure, Goodwill. Right. We could ride bikes."

"I don't have a bike," Luke admitted.

"If you don't mind borrowing my old one, it'll be faster."

Goodwill was empty and quiet when they arrived the next day. An old lady sat behind the cash register wearing dangly earrings that nearly reached her shoulders. She was rearranging trays of costume jewelry.

Luke walked past racks of women's clothes, then racks of men's ties and suit coats. There were bins full of old shoes and scarves. Another of toys. Lumpy couches and tables and chairs and lamps sat crammed together. There was a section of old books and records and wall hangings.

"Do you really think we can find soccer equipment here?" Amelia asked.

"I've never found a ball, but maybe there will be something else."

They set to work digging through the various bins. A truck pulled up and a couple of men started unloading boxes onto the sidewalk. The bell above the door jangled and a group of women came in to shop.

"Hey, Luke," Amelia called. "I found an old soccer jersey. Stuck with the underwear. But it's size eight. For a second grader. Way too small." She balled it up and tossed it back into the bin like she was shooting at a basketball hoop.

Luke laid out several rows of dress shoes and tennis shoes and high-heeled pumps and boots. He matched up the pairs as they came out of the pile. But there was something down at the bottom that felt promising. Luke leaned over, digging deeper. He felt something hard and knobby and tried to pull it up. "There," he grunted, holding up an old cleat. The hard rounded knobs on the bottom were worn, but it was a cleated soccer shoe.

"Hey, those are great!" Amelia said. "Where's the match?"

"At the bottom I hope."

Luke felt like jumping right into the bin. His arms were aching from leaning over and the edges cut into his shoulder.

"Here it is!" Amelia exclaimed and held up the matching shoe triumphantly. "They look a little big. Try them on."

Luke sat down on the floor to remove his shoes. The cleats were large, but not too much.

"You can stuff them with tissues," Amelia suggested.

Shuffling footsteps crossed the hard linoleum floor. It was the elderly lady from the counter. "Children, children," she cried, clapping her hands like a school-teacher. "You mustn't take all the shoes out. Only one pair at a time. This is a terrible mess."

"We'll clean it up," Amelia assured her. "Look, we're picking them all up right now. See?"

"Well," said the lady. "Do a neat, tidy job, please." She returned to her cash register, shooting looks back over her shoulder.

Amelia muttered, "The shoes were in a big jumble to begin with. How do you make a neat, tidy job out of a huge pile?" She poked Luke in the side and laughed.

Luke took the soccer cleats up to the counter. "How much are these?"

The woman plucked at the shoes with thin, mottled fingers and turned them over. There wasn't a price. "Hmm," she murmured. "Eight dollars," she finally said.

"Eight bucks!" Amelia exploded. "Look how worn they are. Won't last more than another season. That's a rip-off."

The old lady harrumphed. "I'm afraid that's the price, young lady. Those kind of shoes are fifty dollars brand-new."

Luke's shoulders sagged. He couldn't ask Mama for that much money. And he only had some loose change back home in his dresser.

He stuffed the shoes back to the bottom of the bin.

"Strikeout!" Amelia declared sadly as they got back onto their bikes. "Luke, those cleats wouldn't have helped you. They were so worn you would have slipped in the first mud puddle on the field. And you're not going to slip if I can help it," she added.

Luke knew she was only trying to make him feel better, but her words almost felt like an ominous warning.

⚽ FIFTEEN

Luke had to forget about the cleats. It was time to put together a team. And the faster the better. Outside the store, he unlocked Amelia's old bicycle, which was chained to a post. "We have to start recruiting. Where do Marcie and Kasey live?"

"Luke," Amelia said, gripping her handlebars and leaping aboard. "You read my mind."

She led the way around the village square and into a residential neighborhood. The houses lay scattered on two-acre lots along a winding gravel road. It looked like a tornado had plunked them down any which way. The road curved and Amelia parked in front of a gray-and-white rectangular house with a long white porch running across the front.

Marcie answered the door in a pale blue sweatshirt and pants. Her black hair had been braided into one long french braid down her back. "Oh, hi. What are you doing? It's cold out there."

Kasey came up behind Marcie. She yawned and peered over Marcie's shoulder.

Marcie said, "We were just about to watch a video."

"We'll make this fast," Amelia told her, nudging Luke in the side.

Luke sucked in his breath. He felt ridiculous, but he was a desperate soccer player. A hopeful, desperate soccer player. "Paul Pickerell wants his soccer team to play our team. We've got a game set up for next Saturday. What position do you want to play?" He didn't want to give her a chance to protest. Just sign them up and start practicing.

Kasey let out a gasp, looking back and forth between Marcie and Luke and Amelia. She started backing away.

"Paul wants to play our *team?*" Marcie repeated. "But we don't have a team."

"We do now," Amelia said cheerfully.

"Hold on," Marcie told her. "Don't get ahead of yourself. You're going to put together a team to play against Paul and Tomás and Mike and all those guys?"

"And we're going to win," Amelia said.

"We'll be lucky if we can even score!" Marcie burst out.

"Think of it this way," Amelia went on, going into a sales pitch. "No girls' team has ever played Paul's team before. We'll be making history. It's what you've always dreamed about."

Marcie considered that. Luke could almost see the wheels in her brain spinning. "It might be fun," she said slowly. "I love watching Paul play. I'd probably love playing with him."

"You mean playing against him," Amelia reminded her.

Marcie smiled again. "Right. Kasey," she called.

Her best friend was fast retreating into the kitchen doorway.

"Kasey, come back," Marcie ordered. "Do you want to play forward or guard?"

"I'm not playing," Kasey said in a low voice.

"Just a minute." Marcie stepped several feet away and grabbed Kasey's arm with a tight grip. They held a consultation, heads bent together.

Luke studied the smooth white trim on the front door. He tried not to look anxious or worried about their verdict.

After a minute Marcie came back. "Kasey thinks we're going to get wiped out."

Luke thought so too, but he wasn't going to say it.

Kasey took a step forward. "You probably want to practice every afternoon for the next week, right? That means I'll be sacrificing my free time."

"What do you do with your free time anyway?" Amelia asked. "Wash your hair?"

Luke wanted to poke her in the arm.

Kasey glared at Amelia. "*And*," she went on, "we'll look like idiots trying to play against the Falcons' team. Am I right or what?"

Luke nodded helplessly. She had it down pretty good.

"What's in it for me?" Kasey demanded.

Luke felt like yelling. Now they had to bribe her?

Amelia narrowed her green eyes like a cat. "What is this, blackmail?"

Marcie laughed. "You're so funny, Amelia. The way we figure it, Paul challenged you to a game and now you're begging us to help you. What do we get out of it?"

Luke thought fast. "There aren't any girl's teams with the *AYSO* league here . . ."

Marcie interrupted. "They don't think there's enough girls who want to play. We have to wait until we get to high school."

Amelia jumped in. "This is our chance to show everybody we're serious about soccer. And maybe we can get our own team. Hey, we could invite some of the league coaches or the president to come watch. Am I brilliant, or what?"

Kasey still looked doubtful, but she glanced at Marcie for direction.

"If you can get Mr. Sanchez, the league officer, there, it's a deal," Marcie said. "I'll play defense and Kasey wants to play goalie."

Amelia looked at the other girl. "You ever been a goalie?"

Kasey shrugged. "Not exactly."

Luke studied Kasey's long, skinny arms. "She can try goalie if she wants. We don't know what position we're good at. None of us have played much on a team before."

Amelia cleared her throat. "Whaddya mean? I played for six years in Montana."

Luke gave her a smile. He was feeling a lot better now. "That's why you're the captain and our coach."

"Oh. Right."

Luke went on before any of the girls could change her mind. "How about meeting at the field after lunch?

Games will be over by then. But we still need another guard and two mid-fielders."

"I'll bet Wendy and Lisa would play. They were on our last team a couple of years ago. I'll call them," Marcie volunteered. "I have their phone numbers."

Luke figured she probably had everybody's telephone numbers. "How about your little sister?" he asked Amelia.

She made a face. "She's only four."

Kasey turned to Marcie. "What about your little sister?"

"You mean Daphne?" Marcie asked. "She's only ten."

"Who else are we going to ask?" Luke didn't know if any of the other girls in their class had ever played.

"Well," Marcie said slowly. "She got her own soccer ball for her birthday last year. And I *have* been working with her lately. She can side-kick pretty good."

Marcie's mother called from the back of the house. "Marcie! Shut the door. We're not heating the outdoors."

"Bring any equipment and balls you have," Luke said quickly.

"Marcie!" Mrs. Gurulé yelled again.

Marcie slammed the front door, and Luke and Amelia got on the bikes.

"My toes are cold," Amelia complained, climbing onto her bike seat. "They could have invited us in."

Luke didn't care about the cold. And he'd never been invited into a house like Marcie's anyway. "I'm just hoping seven people show up later today," he said.

⚽ SIXTEEN

When Luke got home, he had to check on Mr. Perea, who was in bed with the flu. Hurriedly, he fixed the old man a sandwich and a glass of orange juice for lunch.

Mr. Perea spied the blue, scuffed soccer ball sitting by the front door. "Ah, you are off to play the *fútbol.*"

"Got my first game next Saturday," Luke said, peeling him an apple.

"Eh?" Mr. Perea raised his eyebrows. "Did I ever tell you about Ricky's first game at the *universidad?* That man was strong. Big muscles in his thighs. When I saw him, I knew *I* was the amateur. I am never surprised he got with the pros."

"Yeah, you told me," Luke said impatiently. He didn't want to hear about somebody who was probably already dead.

"Get me a glass of water for my pills," Mr. Perea ordered, reaching for a prescription bottle. "Ricky had a move I never tired to see. Ball dribbles up. Center passes to the side. Ricky picks it up and tight dribbles right by the fullbacks. He fakes with the left foot, and shoots with the right. Got it in almost every time."

Luke set down the meal on the bedside table as the elderly man sank onto the bed, looking thin and weak. The sheets were wrinkled and the pillows gray and unwashed. Newspapers and clutter lay heaped everywhere. He handed over the remote control for the television and Mr. Perea waved him away.

"You will not listen about the famous soccer player, no? Another time. I'm tired now, boy."

Luke grabbed his ball, closed the door quietly, and raced along the ditch shortcuts the whole way to the soccer field. His chest was heaving by the time he arrived. And he was late. Someday, he vowed, he was going to be on time for a soccer practice.

Marcie and Kasey and three other girls Luke didn't know were kicking their balls on the grass. It felt strange to go right out on the field and toe his ball, just like he was anybody else.

Wendy was a little chunky and built solid, dressed in soccer shorts and a jersey that was too big. Lisa wore shin guards with a pair of long orange socks expertly folded over that matched her jersey.

"Lisa and Wendy," Amelia said, consulting a clipboard she had brought from home. "You'll both play mid-field. Lisa left center, Wendy right. Marcie and Daphne are defenders—"

Luke glanced at Marcie, who had dressed in matching navy shorts and jersey. She wore shin guards with blue socks, and her shiny black soccer cleats looked brand-new. She popped a ball back and forth on her knees, rarely missing.

Daphne was a miniature version of her older sister, except she had her dark hair tied back with an assortment of red ribbons. She kicked a ball between her feet absentmindedly. But she was dead accurate with that ball.

"Let's warm up!" Amelia yelled. She set down her clipboard and lined them up in two groups. "Since I don't own a personal set of orange cones I used some big rocks for our obstacle course. I set them out over twenty-five yards down the field."

"Where?" Daphne asked. "I don't see them."

Marcie took her sister's arm and pointed out the gray lumps sitting in the grass.

"Dribble the ball around the rocks," Amelia continued. "Weaving in and out and then come back. The next person in your group will go, and we'll keep rotating until everybody's had five turns."

Luke was glad Amelia was in charge. She knew the game, how each position worked, and the strategy of each play. She seemed to love coaching, and he wanted to concentrate on the basics of kicking, dribbling, and passing.

Luke took off for the first rock. He kicked too hard and the ball shot off to the side. He chased it down and dribbled back, trying to ignore the girls' looks. It was tricky to dribble evenly and keep running around each stone.

Marcie beat him to the finish, and Amelia was yelling at everyone. "Good job, keep it moving, way to go Wendy. Don't dribble so wide Daphne, you're not passing it off. That's it! Second round faster now."

By the fifth round Luke had caught up with Marcie.

They finished at an even dead run back to the finish line. Sweat trickled down the sides of his face as he turned to smile at her. Marcie gave him a thumbs-up sign and bent over, breathing hard.

Amelia divided them up in groups of two to try different kicks. Heel kicks, toe kicks, instep kicks, and lob kicks that sent the ball high into the air. During one of the maneuvers, Daphne tripped over a rock and angrily picked it up and threw it downfield. Then Lisa missed her lob kick and accidentally sent the ball straight into Wendy's stomach. Wendy gasped and sat straight down on the field, her face pale. Lisa rushed over to help her up.

Then Marcie tripped over Kasey's feet and they both went sprawling.

"What's the matter with everyone?" Amelia hollered, jumping to her feet. "Haven't you ever played before? I've got a bunch of beginners!"

"Chill out," Marcie told her evenly. "We haven't played together in years. Give us some time."

"We don't have time!" Amelia screeched.

"It is our first practice," Luke reminded Amelia, trying not to let his own frustration show.

"Fine," Amelia said. "Let's practice trapping the ball so we don't get hit in the stomach again. Throw the ball to your partner and have them stop the ball with their chest or leg."

Luke ended up opposite Lisa. She lobbed the ball into the air and he had to lean back to catch it on his chest and stop it. He found it was actually possible to stop the ball with his chest, drop it to the ground, then lob it right back.

Lisa kicked a second time, but the ball was too high. Luke knew he couldn't use his hands to catch it and there wasn't enough time to back up. The next best thing was his forehead to send the ball back. *Whack!* It felt like a hammer had slammed him between the eyes. He fell backward onto the grass with a thudding crash. His eyes crossed and the white, rolling clouds shuddered in the sky above him.

Amelia ran over. "What the heck are you doing, Luke? I haven't taught you that yet."

Luke blinked hard to focus on her face. "I've seen them do that on TV, but it didn't feel too good."

"Okay, since you brought it up, let's try heading the ball." Amelia clapped her hands to get the other girls' attention. "You can intercept a ball with your head and send it back in our team's direction. Keep your head forward and your chin up. Your whole body kind of lunges forward. Whatever you do, don't hit the ball between your eyes like Luke did—"

"Hey! I already figured that out," Luke grunted, rolling over to get up. His head throbbed.

"Sorry, Luke," Amelia told him. "But I need my team to stay healthy."

Now it was *her* team. Oh, well. Luke didn't really care. He just wanted to play. And stay alive on the field when it came time to play Paul.

"Hit the ball high on your forehead, just below your hairline." She demonstrated with Wendy. "Got it? Let's try it now."

Luke kicked the ball to Wendy and she bounced it right back to him with her forehead, snapping her whole body forward. She had good form. He caught the ball and threw it to her again. She got four out of five. Then Wendy threw it to Luke and he tried it. He missed the ball nine times in a row, but on the tenth kick Luke smacked it right at the top of his forehead. The ball whizzed through the air and Wendy trapped it with her chest. On the next one Luke sent it flying over Wendy's head. When he did it right it didn't hurt at all. Kind of a nice wham. It was beautiful watching the ball arc perfectly through the air.

"Good one!" Amelia called from the sideline. "Now we're going to try goal kicks." She lined up the team in front of the net about thirty feet from the line. Then she put Kasey in the center of the goal box. "Kasey, your long arms should be able to grab anything. Only the goalie can touch the ball with her hands," Amelia reminded everyone. "And Kasey—as goalie you can hug the ball, throw yourself on top of it, catch it in the air, anything it takes to stop it from reaching the net. Okay, let's go!"

One at a time they practiced kicking shots into the goal, rotating positions to try different angles. Kasey moved back and forth along the line, hunched over like a tennis player, her face taut and serious. She caught most of the balls, and only had to throw herself to the ground for the ones Amelia or Marcie kicked in.

"Let's spread out on the field now," Amelia ordered. "We have to try passing long distances to each other. Position is very important. If you stay in your field position, we can move the ball around without having to run so much."

"I'm tired," Daphne whined, plopping down on the

grass. Her red ribbons had loosened, hanging down her back like a weary kite tail.

"Amelia's a slave driver," Luke overheard Lisa whisper to Wendy. "This isn't the Olympics or the World Cup."

Wendy nodded. "I thought this game was supposed to be for fun."

"It's not going to be any fun getting slaughtered by the boys," Kasey complained, sidling up on their conversation.

"Okay." Amelia gave in. "Ten-minute break."

The girls straggled over to the sidelines where they had piled up jackets and balls and water bottles. Luke laid down on the grass and closed his eyes, trying to rest his shaking muscles. The grass was cold and slightly damp. He sat up and perched on top of his ball.

Luke considered their situation. If they were going to have any chance against the boys, they had to practice hard like this every day. The girls seemed willing. A moment later his heart sank as two figures crossed the field.

"Hey, bozo!" Paul said, slapping Luke on the back. "Hard workout with the girls, huh? Must be tough. A guy can't keep up."

Behind Paul, Mike laughed. The wind filled his jacket with air, making him look like a football player with shoulder pads.

Luke didn't want to stand up and get in a fight. He gazed past the boys to the road.

"Well, Espinoso, this is your team, huh? A bunch of girls? They look wiped out after a little practice. What're you gonna do when it's time for the real thing?

They'll be begging for mercy after only a couple of plays." Paul hee-hawed and gave Luke another seemingly friendly slap on the shoulder. But he hit hard.

Luke shrugged, wanting to rub his shoulder where Paul had whacked him. He was probably right. They didn't have a prayer. Maybe Mama would pray for them at mass tonight, if that would do any good.

Suddenly, Mike reached out and kicked at Luke's ball.

"Hey!" Luke cried.

Mike kicked again, hard, and the ball popped out, skittering away. Luke fell to the grass on his butt. Mike bent over and grabbed the ball, palming it between his hands. "Grungy ball, Espinoso."

As he stood up, Luke took a ragged breath. "The name's Espinosa. Why don't you try using your ears sometime?"

Mike gave a snort. "Look alive, bozo!" With both hands, he shoved the ball back at Luke, hitting him in the chest. It knocked the breath out of him and Luke gasped, fumbling to keep a grip on the ball, but it fell to the ground. Face burning, he bent over.

"Slippery fingers might not hurt you," Paul said. "But slippery feet in soccer are deadly. See you on the field next week."

"Yeah, probably passed out like we found you today," Mike added.

Paul glanced at Mike out of the corner of his eye. "I don't know, Espinoso," he drawled. "Playing a girl's team is beneath the Fighting Falcons' standards. Maybe we should forget the teams and go back to our original plan. One-on-one, just you and me."

Mike laughed behind his hand, tittering like a third grader.

One-on-one with Paul was the last thing Luke wanted. He wouldn't be ready for that in just a week. Maybe in two or three months. Like maybe next spring's soccer season.

Amelia snapped the lid on her water bottle. "Maybe you don't want to play us, Pickerell. Are you afraid the girls might beat your old Fighting Falcons?"

"Get real!" Paul shot back. "We don't want to hurt all you *girls*," Paul added, eyeing Luke for a rise out of him.

Luke tried to keep from losing his temper. "We'll be ready for you. Next Saturday. Don't worry about that."

"I'm not the one who's worried," Paul said.

Amelia changed the subject. "We need to decide on the game plan. How about ten o'clock?"

"Ten? Sounds good," Paul said. He turned to his friend, smiling. "How is that for you, Mike?"

Mike nodded and grinned back. "Ten is good. Very good."

"We're playing with seven players so you only need to get seven Falcons," Luke added. "Have you told them yet, Pickerell? Are they going to show up?"

"I've got nine Falcons ready to eat you up," Paul retorted.

"But we've only got seven players," Amelia argued. "You can't have substitutions if we can't."

"That's your problem," Paul told her. He yawned and motioned to Mike. They swaggered away and began to try to flirt with the girls. Paul leaned over Marcie. On the sidelines, Lisa and Wendy kicked the ball to each other half-heartedly. Luke stared at Paul, anger oozing up in his gut like a volcano ready to erupt.

Amelia threw down her ball and punted, pretending not to watch the boys. "Why don't they just get lost?" she muttered.

Luke could tell she was bugged. It wasn't good for team morale to have Falcons interrupt practice.

"Break's over," Amelia called. Reluctantly, Marcie broke away from Paul, Daphne tagging behind. Slowly, Lisa and Wendy and Kasey followed.

Daphne's eyes widened as she came up to Luke. "Paul and Mike are so big," she breathed. "We can't play them. They'll run all over us."

"We can do it," Amelia stated, but her voice was flat. "Let's scrimmage a little and get into our playing positions."

"It's been over two hours," Kasey interrupted. "I told my Mom I'd be home by now." She walked away to get her stuff.

"Yeah, I forgot I have to do some things," Marcie remembered. "Come on, Daphne."

Lisa and Wendy spoke up. "We have to go, too. We're supposed to go shopping with our moms."

Within a few moments, the girls were gone.

Luke couldn't blame them. They'd worked hard, and the afternoon was almost gone. But he felt a knot of desperation. This was only the beginning. They had a long way to go.

⚽ SEVENTEEN

Sunday dragged slowly, like a snail crawling up a fence. Luke wanted to call the girls and have another practice. There were only six days until the game.

Luke spent the morning staring at the telephone. He was afraid the girls would hang up on him and tell him to find a new team. In the afternoon he ended up in the bosque with Rex, kicking his ball against the cottonwood until he lost count of how many times he'd kicked it.

On Monday when Luke slid into his school desk he noticed that Amelia's chair was empty. He waited for her to sprint through the door and sling her backpack on her desk, but the bell rang and Mrs. Schaffer stood up for the Pledge of Allegiance. Amelia's seat stayed vacant all day. Luke stared at it through language and spelling and math, wishing he could make her materialize. How could Amelia be absent? He needed her help rallying the girls.

He glanced at Marcie, then Kasey, Lisa, and Wendy over and over, but they were always busy doing school-

work, heads bent over their papers. It was almost like they had never played soccer together.

Paul tried to get Luke's attention several times. Every once in awhile Luke could hear a *psst!* from across the aisle, but Luke carefully ignored him.

It wasn't until after lunch that Luke came up with an idea. Keeping his hands inside his desk, he opened his notebook and quietly ripped out a piece of paper. He tore the paper into four pieces and put them on his desk. Then he wrote out four notes, one to each girl, trying to sound confident and positive.

Don't forget soccer practice today after school. We had a great practice Saturday. We can beat the Falcons!

Luke folded the notes and gave Marcie's to Jeff, who passed it ahead to her, and sent Kasey's sailing across the aisle to her desk. Mrs. Schaffer didn't look up. He didn't think she would suspect him anyway. He had never sent a note in his life.

Luke stood up and went to the pencil sharpener, quickly slipping the other two papers on Lisa and Wendy's desks as he passed. Back at his own desk, he watched the four of them pick up their notes and read them.

Marcie's head lowered and she scribbled furiously. A moment later a folded square sailed backward onto Luke's desk. He opened it. The half page was filled with Marcie's rounded handwriting.

You're serious about this soccer game, aren't you? Saturday was hard and Amelia's a drill sergeant. I don't

know if the girls are going to want to practice like that every day.

Luke wrote back:

We can't practice like wimps and expect to play the Falcons!

We're not going to beat the Falcons, Luke. You're dreaming. We'll be lucky if we can stay on the field for one half.

Luke tore more paper out from his notebook.

Are you willing to try? Think of having an all girls' team next year.

Marcie glanced back at him with a frown.

Yeah, I told you I'd play and I'm not backing out. I guess I'll talk to the other girls. Hint: A bribe might help change their minds.

When Luke read that he almost yelped. These girls wanted his blood. He sat a minute, pondering. He couldn't blame them. They were doing him the favor. He pencilled another note and tossed it back to Marcie.

I'll throw them a party, cake and ice cream, if we score against the Falcons. That's my best offer.

Great! Where will the party be?

Luke grinned. That was easy. He wrote:

Your house.

Marcie's shoulders shook with laughter and she pressed down on her pencil.

You drive a hard bargain. It's a deal.

After the last note, Luke glanced up. Marcie looked over her shoulder, giving him a little thumbs-up sign.

Mrs. Schaffer cleared her throat. "Miss Gurulé? Mr. Espinosa? Have you finished your paper chat?"

Luke jerked his head up, his face burning at being caught. He looked down at his desk, which was littered with notes. They *had* written quite a few.

"Way to go, Espinoso," Paul hissed across the aisle.

Mrs. Schaffer peered at Luke over her glasses. "May I have those notes, please?"

Marcie seemed rooted to her chair. Slowly, Luke stood up and gathered the slips on his desk and the notes on Marcie's desk. He dumped them on the teacher's desk.

"Quite a conversation," Mrs. Schaffer observed, riffling through the pile of paper notes. "Please finish reading your chapter and from now on, wait until recess to converse."

At lunchtime, Luke collected the notes from Mrs. Schaffer's desk and put them in his backpack. He didn't want any Falcons to get hold of them.

After the final afternoon bell rang, Marcie retrieved Daphne from the fourth-grade hall, and the team met at the fields. Lisa lived close by and ran home for a couple of balls. She also called Amelia's house.

"Amelia's sick," Lisa announced when she returned. "Strep throat."

"Too much yelling at us on Saturday," Kasey said.

Luke bit his tongue to keep from snapping at her. "We need her. She's the most experienced out of all of us and our best player."

"I'm good, too," Marcie said, hands on her hips.

"Hey," Luke said quickly. "I think all of you are great. We better get practicing."

"And it's going to be dark in an hour," Wendy reminded everybody.

That was the problem with November. It was getting dark by five-thirty. Practice didn't go much better that day. Somehow, without Amelia, their numbers felt even smaller than six. Luke led them through the same drills that Amelia had outlined Saturday, and tried to stay positive, but it was the hardest thing he'd ever had to do. Too soon it was dark and everyone left for home, bundled up in their coats. A chill wind swept down through the valley from the Manzano Mountains. Luke jogged along the darkening streets, hoping Amelia would get better fast. He didn't know how long strep throat lasted.

The next day, school couldn't go by fast enough, Luke was so anxious to get to the soccer fields. He wished there weren't any school at all. Then they could practice all day long. There was so much to practice and not enough time.

After school, they met in the bosque. The cottonwoods had lost most of their leaves and the branches looked like bare, bony skeleton arms twisted together. It was colder by the river and they had to run harder to stay warm, but they were good practices. And private. Without the prying eyes of Paul and Mike or any other Falcons.

On Wednesday Luke divided them into two teams of three and they practiced playing a game. By the end of the afternoon Luke was desperate for Amelia. They couldn't play with just six team members. And he was never meant to coach.

When he got home after dark, Luke kicked the ball through the house and down the hall. He felt fidgety and couldn't seem to sit still.

He went to the phone and called information for Amelia's telephone number.

Her mother answered, sounding doubtful about letting her talk to him. But suddenly Amelia's hoarse voice came over the line. "I can talk, Mom. Hi, Luke."

"You sound terrible," he told her.

"Thanks a lot," Amelia shot back.

"Are you going to be able to play on Saturday?" he asked.

"Of course. I'm planning to be at practice tomorrow, if my mother doesn't chain me to the bed."

Luke laughed. "Don't end up in the hospital or something."

"Me? No way. But I better get back to bed now so I can get out tomorrow."

Until Mama got home from work, Luke kicked and bounced the ball around the trailer until he dropped onto the couch, exhausted.

"Are you ready to play on Saturday?" she asked him,

setting down her coat and purse. "Will the boys give you any extra time?"

"Paul's so anxious to play he spends most of the day grinning at me," Luke told her, sighing.

Mama smiled sympathetically and sank into a chair. "Well son, I got brave and made two phone calls today myself."

Luke sat up.

"At the end of November, there is a scheduled GED test I can take in the city."

"That's good," Luke told her.

"I hope I will be ready," she said, making a cross in the air. "I'm so nervous, but I'm getting better at the study booklet. Plus, I called a beauty school, too. They're taking new students in January."

"You have enough money saved, then?" Luke eagerly asked.

"Enough for the first part," his mother said, and gave him a hopeful smile. "They told me to come in and fill out an application for student aid or scholarship. I might be able to get one. I thought scholarships were just for regular college." She covered her face with her hands for a moment, then looked at him again. "Luke, it might really happen. After so long, it's hard to believe."

He knew just what she meant. "It will happen, Mama. I know it."

On Thursday Amelia was back on the field, wearing a thick woolen scarf around her neck. "My mother made me wear this thing. It was the only way I could get out of the house. And I can only play for an hour.

Not a minute more. Period. At least, that's how she put it."

It was so good to see her, Luke almost felt like hugging her. "Are you better?"

She brushed her hair out of her eyes. "I'm still on medicine until next Monday, but I feel a lot better and I'm not contagious anymore. Let's play ball."

"We need a name for our team," Luke said as they laid out on the ground doing stretching exercises.

Marcie bent in half, touching her nose to her knee like an aerobics teacher. "How about calling ourselves the Cheetahs? We're fast like a cheetah."

"You mean the Elephants," grumbled Kasey.

"Speak for yourself," Marcie snapped back. "We're not going to stand up to the boys if we keep thinking like that."

"Marcie's right," Luke put in. He was relieved to hear her confidence, and hoped it would rub off on the other girls.

"What about being the Eagles?" Wendy asked. "You know, we soar over the field."

Lisa shook her head. "It sounds too much like the Falcons."

"True," Amelia agreed. "I like something mysterious and unpredictable. My grandma's favorite international team is the Pumas. Let's be the Pumas."

Luke clenched his teeth, but didn't say anything.

Amelia gave him a quick glance.

"What the heck does Puma mean?" Daphne asked, wrinkling her nose.

Amelia jumped in. "It means Panther. Let's be the Panthers instead. They're sly and cunning and sneak up on their prey. That will fit us. The boys will never know what hit 'em."

"Let's vote on it," Marcie said. "Everyone who wants to be the Panthers say Aye."

There was a chorus of "Ayes!"

"Yeah, Panthers!" Amelia shouted, jumping up. "Let's play soccer!"

Luke knew he was finally getting better. He could kick the ball harder and farther than a month ago when he first found his ball. He could run the field without getting winded. But then, he'd been running the ditch banks for years. Now he could dribble the ball from goal to goal without losing it to another player, except Amelia once in awhile. He'd netted a few goals, too, but Kasey was getting better at catching them. When she wasn't complaining about getting wiped out, she made a good goalie.

But the days were quickly wearing away. The game was coming too close, too soon. On Friday the practice was awful. Balls ricocheted off legs and arms. Luke thought he'd never chased down so many. Amelia kept banging on her forehead every time something went wrong, and trying not to scream at everybody.

Finally Marcie said, "This is no good."

"Yeah," agreed Kasey. "I'm sick of getting drilled on the same stuff over and over, and getting hit in the stomach."

Luke stuck his hands on his hips. "Let's just go home and get some sleep before tomorrow." He watched the girls straggle off, except for Amelia who barreled across the field toward him.

"Why'd you do that?" she shouted. "I'm the Panther captain!"

"Sorry, but we can't do anymore," Luke said.

Amelia shook her head. "Another month and we could beat those old Falcons."

Luke couldn't even think about it.

"I hope the principal shows up," Amelia went on. "Yesterday Marcie and I invited him to our game. He said the board has been talking about organizing some girls' teams for the spring. If he sees how good we are that will help clinch it for us."

Marcie walked up to them. "I just heard the latest on Paul's brother, Phil. He didn't make the cut this year for the team. They told him to try again next season."

Amelia shook her head. "Paul's going to be in a terrible mood tomorrow. We're going to need eyes in the back of our heads."

That night Luke felt sick. It was hard to sleep. Shadows from the streetlight flickered back and forth across the ceiling as he lay in his hammock, twisting the worn leather ball in his lap. He didn't know what time it was when he got up and dug out the letter from Ricardo Espinosa from his dresser.

He read it again for the first time since the day he received it. The man was a stranger to him. They were flesh and blood, but they were strangers. And his father had treated him like he might some kid on the street.

Ricardo Espinosa had passed on the longing to play soccer somewhere in his blood. For Luke, it had become his dream. But that was all his father had passed on. Maybe it was Mama who'd given him determination.

Tomorrow, he would take the best of both of them and play better than he ever had.

He hugged the blue ball to his chest, then let the letter slip through his fingers to the floor.

⚽ EIGHTEEN

Luke woke early. It was chilly, the skies an overcast gray. But no sign of clouds or snow. Good soccer weather.

He fastened Amelia's old shin guards over his calves and pulled up the long blue socks Mama had splurged to buy him. He studied the tread on the bottoms of his sneakers and decided they were good enough. They had to be. Maybe by spring he could find a way to buy cleats. After he finished dressing, Luke went into the kitchen and fixed a piece of toast.

Mama shuffled down the hall, yawning. "It is too early after working until two A.M., but I wanted to say good luck, baby. I hope you win."

Luke set his milk glass in the sink. "We're not going to win, Mama. I'll be glad if we can score at least once."

"You will do wonderful," Mama whispered in his ear as she hugged him.

"Don't come to the field and watch," Luke told her. "If I ever make it on a team you can come then."

"I'm not planning on watching and making you nervous. I have the morning off and I am baking your celebration cake for your party."

Startled, Luke looked at her. He'd been worrying about how to get a cake. Of course, it was very possible the Falcons would cream them and they wouldn't need a cake at all. "How did you know about the party?"

Mama smiled. "It was easy to figure out when you dropped some notes out of your school pack. I think they were from a girl named Marcie?"

"Oh yeah," Luke muttered. "I got Rosie to get me two cartons of ice cream from Ramon at the dairy."

"You can't have ice cream without cake. Now you are going to be late, *hijo*." She stood at the door and waved to him.

Luke jogged to the field along the ditch bank, slowly warming up. He breathed the cold air deeply and evenly to prevent an ache in his side.

As soon as he reached the field Amelia ran up, moaning. "We're skunked, Luke. Paul pulled a fast one. It's all my fault. I forgot all about it."

Her panic scared him. "What do you mean? What'd we forget?"

"We needed a referee and we forget to ask a teacher or a parent or *somebody* from the league."

"Oh, man," Luke exhaled, his mind racing ahead.

She grimaced. "Paul is one step ahead of us. Guess who he got? Tomás's older brother. This guy's going to call the plays in favor of them and against us."

"Let me think," Luke said.

Players from both teams had begun to arrive and started to run around the perimeter of the field to warm up. Coach Pickerell dropped off Paul and got out of the car himself.

"Dad, please don't stay," Paul hissed as Luke passed to join the long, snaky line of runners.

"Why not? I want to see how you do against a bunch of girls." The man laughed.

Luke cringed. What had Paul told his dad?

"Go home," Paul said in a hard, low voice.

"Okay, son. I'll do that," Mr. Pickerell said stiffly. "But you cream them. Don't let them score. Not even once. I want a full report of the game when you get home."

Paul didn't reply. He stared at his father, then turned and raced past Luke to join his team.

Coach Pickerell's words repeated in Luke's mind as he jogged the field. He tried to shake them away, but he couldn't. Was there stuff about Paul he didn't know? Maybe the daydreams he had about Paul and his father weren't even right. It was a strange thought and he looked at Paul with new eyes. Maybe there were other reasons Paul got so obnoxious about his soccer status.

Today wasn't the day to get soft on Paul. He had to keep his head clear. As Luke ran, he scouted out the players. There were fourteen. Seven for each side. Paul grinned at Luke, his thin face bright with anticipation. His dad's words didn't seem to have any lasting effect, but perhaps Paul was just good at hiding it.

Like the wind, Tomás Abeyta flew past, his long, black hair fluttering over his shoulders. Tomás's brother Henry ran next to him. He was about seventeen and Luke had seen him coaching and refereeing for the district. A boy could take refereeing classes and get certified when he turned fourteen. Perhaps he'd do that in a couple of years.

The two brothers slowed down and Luke fell back so he wouldn't run into them. Tomás glanced over his shoulder and gave Luke a brief nod. There was never the same challenging look in Tomás's eyes as in Paul's. He was here to play soccer because he loved the sport, nothing else.

Henry stopped to lean over and breathe. "Hey," he said to Luke.

"Hey," Luke replied, looking into the older boy's face for some kind of reassuring sign. But his face was as unemotional as Tomás's usually was.

Henry lifted his chin toward Luke. "You guys are brave to play against the Falcons. They finished their season nine-one."

"Gee, thanks," Luke told him.

Henry gave a little laugh. "Sorry. I wasn't trying to scare you. Only impressed that you're willing."

Luke finished his lap and searched for Amelia. He couldn't do anything about the ref problem. He'd never seen Tomás play dirty, and he wasn't part of Paul's group. Luke had to hope Henry was the same. Besides, the game was about to start. If they backed out now, he'd look scared or like he was making excuses not to play.

Amelia jogged up and Luke took her aside. "It's our own fault we don't have a choice about who refs."

"But Luke," Amelia protested.

"There's nothing we can do now," Luke said. "We'll have to take our chances and hope Abeyta will call the plays fairly."

Amelia looked doubtful, but said, "If you say so."

As the Panthers huddled together, Luke scanned their faces. Solemn, serious, and nervous. But hopeful and ready to play hard. It was a good sign.

"Hang tough, Daphne," Amelia said, giving everyone last-minute pointers. "They're bigger, but you can be quicker. Keep the ball moving, watch out for fouls. Marcie, send us your long kicks so Luke and I can score. Lisa and Wendy, watch for the interceptions. They'll steal in a split second. Kasey, stay awake in that goal box and grab everything. You control the ball the minute it enters your goal box. Then pass the ball out to the side, never kick it to the center. The main thing is to keep control of the ball! We can hold 'em zero-zero if they can't get that ball in the net."

Kasey nodded tightly at Amelia's words, shivering in the cool morning air.

Henry Abeyta called for the lineup, and a minute later the players had spread out on their respective sides of the field.

"Luke," Amelia said. "This is your game, buddy. Get in there."

Luke didn't look at Paul while he positioned himself opposite the Falcon captain in the center circle. The girls scattered behind him, ready.

Henry raised his voice to be heard over the field. "We'll play one half since there's no substitutes. If we don't, you'll all be dead at the end."

Paul smiled at Luke. "You'll be dead anyway."

Henry gave him a stern gaze. "We'll flip a coin to see who starts." He pulled out a quarter. "Heads or tails, Luke?"

"Heads."

Henry tossed the coin into the air and caught it on the back of his hand. "Heads it is. Panthers' ball."

Luke sucked in his breath. Every muscle in his body was tight. He wished he could run another lap to relax, but this was it.

Paul flicked his chin into the air. "Espinoso, I see you got a midget playing defense."

Luke shot a quick glance back at Daphne over his shoulder. She looked fine. Ready for play. He turned back just as Henry blew his whistle and put the ball on the dewy grass.

Paul laughed, knowing he'd distracted Luke. Luke fumbled for the ball and kicked at it clumsily, trying to get it sideways to Amelia, but Paul was incredibly quick. A few rapid steps and the Falcon captain had stolen it away. Paul kicked it down center toward the goal box.

The Falcons charged after it for a quick score, but Wendy was ready and ran up to the ball to head it off. Paul had kicked high and as the ball arced down through the air, she jumped up to intercept, smacking it with the top of her head. It was a hard hit and Wendy fell over as the ball bounced toward Lisa, who booted it back across the midline.

Luke glanced over his shoulder to make sure Wendy wasn't hurt as he caught the ball with his toe and began to dribble downfield. He saw Paul nearly explode as he watched his team lose control of the ball. At the Falcon goal box, a big, husky kid loped back and forth waiting for Luke.

Suddenly, Falcons swarmed him from both sides.

Legs kicked, trying to steal the ball. Luke caught sight of Amelia open for a pass and lobbed the ball to her. She chest-trapped it and kept dribbling. But she was off-center and stuck on the sidelines. Falcon guardsmen were all over her. Luke raced over to open up for a pass. Amelia spotted him and kicked it out, but a guard intercepted and booted the ball away from Luke. Instantly, another Falcon guard kicked it back to the Falcon side.

Paul caught the ball with his thigh and dribbled right by Lisa and Wendy. He sideswiped Daphne and passed it to Mike. Marcie and Daphne raced after him, but a second later Mike had passed it back to Paul. Side by side, the two boys sent the ball shooting back and forth between each other. The Panthers tried to intercept in vain. The two boys laughed. It was like a keep-away game. The ball crept closer toward the goal.

Kasey was shaking, her face pale. She ran back and forth, arms outstretched, trying to predict where the kick was going to come from. Suddenly, Paul whammed the ball with the top of his foot. It sailed hard for the net. Kasey jumped for it. She fell to the earth, burying the ball underneath her chest.

The Panthers screamed.

"Way to go, Kasey!" Amelia yelled.

Kasey rose, hugging the ball as if she was afraid someone would take it away from her.

Luke noticed Paul kicking the dirt and swearing under his breath at Kasey's catch. "Boot it," Luke shouted to her. "Boot it out of there!" Quick kicking by the goalie would get the ball to the opposite side of the field so that he and Amelia could try scoring before the rest of the Falcons could run back and defend.

But Kasey was dazed and slow to react. She dropped the ball and kicked it, but the Falcons had quickly dispersed into position and were ready.

"That's okay, Kasey," Luke shouted. "You stopped the goal, that's what counts."

Marcie managed to tag the ball and send it swiveling off to the side, away from the center. Daphne raced after it, but the ball rolled out of bounds.

Henry blew the whistle and scooped up the ball. "Falcon throw-in." Tomás stepped out and took the ball from his brother. Henry blew the whistle again and Tomás threw the ball over his head to Paul.

Paul picked it up smoothly and dribbled to the center for another attempt at the goal. Kasey was out in front, criss-crossing across the goal box. Marcie and Daphne were all over Paul, trying to steal. He turned and turned again, successfully keeping it away. His eyes roved the goal box looking for a break to drive it in. Lisa and Wendy, the mid-fielders, sprinted to help. But in a flash Paul passed to his teammate. The ball danced across the grass and Tomás scooped it up with his foot. A split second later Tomás kicked it across the goal line.

Kasey couldn't get to the other side of the goal box in time. She leaped for the ball, but missed and fell flat on the grass. The ball bounced into the net. One point for the Falcons.

The boys' team jumped into the air, whooping and hollering. Paul and Mike slapped hands triumphantly.

The Panthers bent over to catch their breath. Luke

shook his head, hardly able to believe his eyes. It had been a whirlwind goal.

The Falcons had definitely warmed up. Even though the Panthers got the next kickoff, a Falcon mid-fielder immediately snagged it up and gained control. Within moments the Falcon player passed and the boys had the ball down at the goal again, setting up for another shot. Just as Tomás passed again, Paul ran forward, whacked the ball and sent it straight into the net. The Panthers groaned at the second point. Scored even faster than the first.

Amelia started the next kickoff, but Mike quickly stole it, heading straight for Kasey again. Anxious to prevent the Falcons from scoring again, Lisa and Wendy rushed into Mike just as he swung his foot into the ball.

Henry blew the whistle. "Foul on you. Charging," he said, pointing at Lisa.

"Hey, no way, no fair," Amelia yelled across the field. "Foul? I didn't see any foul."

"Free kick," Henry called.

Luke went up to Amelia. "It's true. Lisa bumped Burrell as he tried to score."

"You're positive?"

"I'm sure," Luke told her.

The Panthers had to stand back, helpless, as Mike positioned the ball where he wanted it. He backed up a few steps and attacked the ball, kicking hard. The ball sailed right over Kasey's head and sank into the net. The Panthers groaned as the Falcons cheered again, even louder than before.

"Three-nothing, Falcons," Henry said. "Panthers start the next play."

Luke ran to center field.

Henry placed the ball on the grass and Luke gave it a swift thud to the side. It arced and Amelia caught it with her leg and began dribbling down the sidelines. She and Luke passed it back and forth, moving it down the field. But it didn't last. Paul flashed in front of Luke and with one quick move he'd stolen the ball. Luke scrambled to get it back. Minutes ticked by as the ball went back and forth between the two teams. Five times it was kicked out of bounds and thrown back in.

Over and over Amelia managed to get the ball into Falcon territory, but she couldn't seem to close in on the goal. Several times she got it within a few feet to try and score, but the Falcons knew she was the Panthers' best player and swarmed her constantly, stealing the ball. Luke glanced at Amelia. She had a fierce, determined look on her face, while he had an ache in his gut the size of a boulder. His legs burned as if they were on fire. And the clock was running out.

Henry gave a blast on the whistle. First quarter.

Luke gulped in air. It was a hard, fast game. The Panthers grouped together, all breathing heavily.

Marcie rubbed her hands on her thighs. She was silent. Luke couldn't tell what she was thinking.

Kasey moaned, "This is awful. We're getting creamed."

"We're not getting creamed!" snapped Amelia. "They'd be creaming us if they had ten points, not three."

"Okay," Luke said, "Let's all just relax. I think everybody is playing great. We still have a chance. There's half the game left. We're holding the Falcons pretty good."

"I don't call three to zero holding 'em," Daphne said.

"You want to quit now and forfeit?" Amelia asked.

Luke looked at Wendy and Lisa and Daphne. Then he caught Marcie and Kasey's eyes. They all shook their heads. Nobody was ready to give up yet.

"I want to stop some more goals," Kasey said solemnly. Then she laughed.

Marcie smiled at her friend, then at Luke. "I'm not sure we'll ever score, but it's a good game. There's no way I want to quit now."

Luke started to smile back when Daphne shaded her eyes and pointed across the field. "Who are those people over there?"

A dented yellow Chevy slowly pulled alongside the sidewalk, a coat of mud staining its chrome fenders. The front tires hit the concrete curb and the driver squealed the brakes, abruptly stopping the vehicle, but the big old car swayed from the impact. The engine cut.

"Oh man," breathed Luke. It was Rosie. He recognized Ramón's car.

⚽ NINETEEN

The ancient Chevy doors groaned on their hinges and Mr. Perea unfolded his legs from behind the dash. He was bundled up in a jacket and knitted cap, a red scarf around his neck. Wearing the green windbreaker and sneakers without socks, Rosie bent over to unfasten her baby from the car seat. She hitched him up on her hip and waved. "Yoohoo! Hey, Luke!"

"*Who* are they?" Kasey asked.

Hands on her hips, Amelia bent over, staring. "I'm not sure. I think they live at the trailer park."

Luke wanted to sink into the grass. "They're my neighbors," he muttered.

Mr. Perea opened the back door of the car, and Old Rex cautiously jumped out and followed his master as the old man shuffled across the grass. Rosie held the baby in her right arm and took the old man's elbow with her other arm. "Surprised, Luke?" Rosie asked with a big grin.

"What are you doing here?" Luke asked, glancing self-consciously at all the players on the field.

"Well, Mr. Perea was feeling better and came over

to my place—" Her baby drooled on her hand and she wiped it on her jeans. "And Ramón said it was okay to let me use the car if we came right back and I said—"

Mr. Perea held up a wrinkled hand to stop Rosie's chatter. He cleared his throat. "Old Rex has been barking all morning—never see him do this before. He knows we have to come. But now I shut up. You have a game to play, Luke Espinosa. *Qué no?*"

Luke looked into the old man's black eyes. Then he glanced down. One of the ancient, brown leather soccer balls was clutched in the crook of Mr. Perea's arm. "*Verdad,*" he said, rubbing his hands across Rex's saggy head. "I have a game to play."

He ran out to the field. Marcie and Lisa and Amelia all looked at him, questions on their faces. He just shrugged. But suddenly, he felt good. And he couldn't figure out exactly why.

"Hey, look at that!" Amelia said, pointing. Another car had pulled up behind Rosie's yellow Chevy. A blue Volvo. At the wheel sat Mr. Sanchez, and another man from the league in the passenger side. Amelia raised her hand triumphantly to Marcie.

It was the Falcons' ball. A mid-fielder threw it in and another Falcon half-back butted it downfield again. Right into the center. Paul was ready. He picked up the ball with his foot and slid it right past Kasey into the corner of the net. Just like that, the Falcons had four points. Luke's moments of feeling good suddenly disappeared. His shoulders slumped and he bent over, hands on his knees. The game was slipping farther away, and there was nothing they could do.

Amelia ran over and thumped him sternly on the back. "Game's not over yet."

He shook his head. "I don't think we can recover."

Amelia looked like she wanted to strangle him. "Pull out of it, Luke."

"Panthers' ball," Henry said after the Falcons had stopped cheering their new goal.

Paul hooted with laughter. "Why don't you give up, Espinoso?"

Henry cut him down with a sharp glance. "Stifle it, Pickerell."

"Huddle, huddle," Amelia ordered quickly. She bent her head to the middle, talking low. "The clock's running out. This is our last chance. I want to move all our players down, even the guards."

"Who's going to defend the goal and help Kasey out?" Marcie demanded. "That's too risky."

"We have to risk it," Luke told them, agreeing with Amelia. "We have nothing to lose. Sure, if the ball gets kicked past Kasey again, they'll score. Another point won't matter. But without everybody down there we can't score ourselves."

"Got it?" Amelia asked.

"Yeah," Marcie said, wiping her forehead with her shirt. "I see what you mean."

"Everyone pick a man to guard," Amelia directed. "Try to keep them from passing. Wendy, you're accurate on throw-ins. You throw the ball to Luke. The rest of us will guard our player and give Luke a shot at getting near the goal."

The whistle sounded impatiently.

But Amelia paused and stuck her hand in the center

of the tight cluster. Luke followed her lead, then the rest of the team reached out and they all joined hands. "Go-o-o-o Panthers!" They shot their arms into the air.

Luke clapped his hands together, adrenalin making his pulse race. He ignored the snickers coming from the Falcons and concentrated on the play ahead of them.

The Panthers scattered into position, guarding their assigned man. Wendy threw the ball over her head to Luke. He trapped it and turned to dribble. One of the Falcon guards was on his tail, but Amelia ran in to cut him off. She followed Luke, arms up, keeping the other players away so he could run the ball.

Out of the corner of his eye, Luke saw that Paul and Mike had been caught by Lisa and Marcie. Wendy was all over Tomás and Daphne was trying to keep up with the other guard.

"Keep going, Luke," Amelia whispered fiercely. "You got it."

His lungs burned and his legs tingled from fatigue, but Luke kept his eye on the ball. In front of him, the goalie moved back and forth. He had to time his kick just right to place the ball past the goalie when he moved sideways for that split second.

A foot darted in to steal. Another foot. Luke kept dribbling, praying he wouldn't trip.

Suddenly, Amelia fell back, caught by a Falcon. Paul raced over, arms pumping, a grin all over his face. Marcie and Lisa were left in the dust.

Then Luke saw his opening. He had it! Paul was right behind him, but if he kicked now it would be too late for the Falcon captain to intercept. It was now or never. Luke reared back to give the ball a mighty whack. At the same moment, Paul slid across the grass, and swept Luke's legs out from under him. Arms flailing, Luke crashed to the ground. The ball skittered off to the side and the Falcon goalie picked it up. Instantly the goalie booted it down the field before Luke could even stand up again.

Henry blew his whistle. Nobody paid any attention. The Falcons raced downfield with the ball, charging toward the goal. Before the Panthers knew what was happening, Mike drove the ball past Kasey. She clawed the air trying to stop the goal, but the ball hit the back of the net.

The Falcons yelled, slapping hands, leaping into the air.

Henry screamed on his whistle until he was red. He waved his arms canceling out the play. "No good. No goal. I called a foul on Paul and everybody ignored me. Sweeping a player is illegal. And it was on a goal shot. Luke gets a penalty kick."

Mike and Paul cupped their mouths, booing Henry. Paul stuck a hand in Henry's face, yelling, "Luke ran into *me*. We got five points."

Henry looked him straight in the face, his lips thin. "The fifth goal is no good. You were sweeping that player. That's the most illegal move in the book."

"You don't know nothing," Paul argued back.

Tomás stepped in front of him. "My brother's right and you know it."

"Get out of my way, Abeyta," Paul said. Anger heated his face. He shoved Tomás with both arms and stalked off.

Luke rose slowly. His ankle had twisted when he

went down. That sweeping move from Paul—he hadn't seen it coming at all. Stupid. He should have anticipated Pickerell doing something like that.

Henry bent over and looked Luke in the eye. "You okay to kick?"

Luke tested his foot. "Yeah, I'm okay." It was his left foot that had buckled, not his kicking foot. But he walked cautiously to the center in front of the goal box.

Now it was just him against the goalie. The two teams had to stand back and watch. Luke placed the ball on the grass and the referee blew one short toot.

"Any time you're ready," Henry called.

The goalie swayed back and forth, feet planted on the front line.

Luke knew he couldn't drive it straight in. The goalie would snag it for sure. He stepped back several feet, turning his body at an angle. He was going to make it look like he planned to shoot right. The goalie wavered to that side, arms out.

Luke wiped his brow. The field swam in front of his eyes. The goalie seemed huge, thick arms and legs all over the goal box. The net was tiny and far away. He shut his eyes, fear paralyzing him.

From the sidelines, he heard Amelia yell, "You can do it, Luke! Just like the cottonwood tree. Twenty times in a row."

Old Rex suddenly got to his feet, head up, eyes on Luke. He barked once sharply, tail thumping the air. That's all Luke needed. He opened his eyes, and suddenly the corner of the net became the old, gnarled cottonwood in the clearing.

Luke ran forward. When he reached the ball he

caught it with his instep, driving it off to the left instead of the right, and smacking as much punch into it as he could. It was a difficult move to kick hard, but he was close enough to the goal to make it possible.

Too late, the Falcon goalie realized it was a fake. He reversed directions and lunged back, but missed the ball by a fraction of an inch. The soccer ball skimmed across the green sea of grass and cruised right into the corner. The net ate it.

Luke let out his breath with a whoosh and almost laughed out loud. He didn't think anything could feel so good as watching the net sink his ball. One beautiful point for the Panthers!

Behind him, Amelia and Marcie and the other girls shrieked, their yells blasting the air. Wendy slapped his shoulder and Daphne was shaking his arm.

"*Whooee!* You did it, Luke," Amelia shouted.

"We got a point!" screamed Daphne.

Henry blew the whistle again. "Time's up. Falcons four, Panthers one. Good game." He gave a little smile. "Catch you kids later. I'm outta here."

At the sidelines, every Panther was yelling with joy. Wendy and Lisa hugged each other. Luke watched Amelia running the ball in a circle and grinning like crazy. Her whole body looked happy. "Hey, Luke, great shot. Where's that party you promised? And did you see those men from the league? Maybe I won't go back to Montana after all."

Luke laughed. "We'll meet at Marcie's in an hour. I'm going home to get the ice cream. My mom's baking a cake, too."

"See you there!" Amelia ran off to get her coat and water bottle.

From the Falcon side of the field, Tomás slung his jacket over his shoulders, picked up his ball, and came over to Luke. "Good game, Espinosa. You should try out for the team this spring."

Luke nodded. "Thanks, I think I will." He looked down at the grass for a moment, working up his courage. "We're having a party in a little while at Marcie's if you'd like to come."

"You're inviting a Falcon to a Panther party?" Tomás asked.

"Sure, why not?" Luke said, looking him in the eye.

Tomás nodded. He didn't exactly smile, but he looked pleased. "I can probably make that." Then he lifted his hand in farewell and headed toward the road.

A second later Rosie rushed up. "What an exciting game!" she said, squeezing Luke's arms.

Mr. Perea harrumphed and stopped in front of Luke, running his hands down the front of his coat. "Potential, boy. You have that, I will tell you. A few more years and you might be like Ricky, the soccer player who lived next to me once. Have I told you about him? He liked to fake the goalie."

"Yeah, you've told me about him," Luke said. "Hey, Mr. Perea. Whatever happened to him? Did you know him in Mexico before you came to the States?"

The old man pulled himself up indignantly. "I have been here for fifty years, I will tell you."

"Well, didn't Ricky live about fifty years ago?"

"No, I tell you he lived next door. At Rio Grande Trailer Park. He was good, he was."

"Come on, Mr. Perea," Rosie said, nudging him. "The baby's cold. And your lips are turning blue."

"My lips are never blue," the old man told her tersely, but he allowed Rosie to take his arm as they walked back to the old Chevy.

Luke watched their slow steps as Mr. Perea's words sank in. He felt stupid for not knowing who Ricky was all this time. It should have been so obvious. Then he heard a snicker behind him.

"Friends of yours?" Paul laughed, jerking a thumb at the backs of Rosie and Mr. Perea.

Luke looked the other boy square in the eye. "Yes, they are my friends," he told Paul, and he felt proud to say it. Everything was good. It was a good day, and only just beginning.

Paul edged closer. "A penalty kick is a giveaway point, Espinoso," he cracked. "Easy shot. That baby Daphne could have done it."

Luke swung around. He'd had it. "Pickerell," he shot back. "Nobody gave me nothing. Except maybe you. You knew I was going to score and the only way to stop me was to sweep. Next time take your chances with the real thing instead of cheating."

Paul grabbed Luke by the sweatshirt. "Watch who you're calling a cheater, Espinoso. And there won't be a next time. I can fix it with my dad so you never play soccer again."

Mike ran up and flung his arm around Paul's neck, punching him in the stomach. "Good game, buddy. We did it again. And this year our tournament team is going to the state championships. It's going to be great!"

"Shut up, Mike," Paul told his friend. "Espinoso, we wiped you off the field."

Luke shrugged and turned a slow smile on him. He owned this moment and Paul couldn't take it away. The best part was, Paul knew it, too. "Hey, Paul!" he called. "Next spring, buddy." Luke gave him the thumbs-up sign.

Paul scowled and walked away.

Luke could only smile inside, although part of him felt funny, like his eyes were going to start watering. But he wasn't even sure what he'd be crying for. He'd played better than he ever had.

One thing he did know was that he didn't care what the Falcon captain did or said anymore. By spring soccer season Luke would be ready for Paul or anybody else. He had his room set up for practice all winter. Even his father had left him a legacy, though Ricardo Espinosa didn't know it. Would never know it. But that was going to be his loss, not Luke's. He couldn't feel jealous of Paul anymore, and he couldn't feel sorry for him, either. Just like Luke, Paul had to find his own way.

Luke went over to the sidelines and grabbed his ball with the scuffed blue hexagons. Old Rex sat waiting for him, panting with his tongue hanging out. Luke pulled on his jacket that was getting too small and tucked the soccer ball into the crook of his arm. It fit perfectly, like a good friend. Old Rex got to his feet, then Luke slowly jogged home along the ditch banks. The pale November skies were turning warm and blue.